WHO STOLE MY TIME?

Reclaiming our lives from the social media trap

WHO STOLE MY TIME?

Reclaiming our lives from the social media trap

SUNIL MISHRA

PAPER TOWNS
PUBLISHERS

PAPER TOWNS
PUBLISHERS

First published by
Papertowns Publishers
72, Vishwanath Dham Colony,
Niwaru Road, Jhotwara,
Jaipur, 302012

Who Stole My Time?
Copyright © Sunil Mishra, 2020

ISBN Print Book - 978-93-87131-72-9

Printed in India

Preface

Are we using our smartphones today, or are our smartphones using us? I would certainly like to believe the former but unknowingly we all slip into the latter category. If by reading this story, one can critically examine their relationship with social media and reset it, the objective of the book would be partly met.

With numerous digital technologies around, we can do so many things at the click of the button. Ideally, this should have given us so much free time in our lives. On the contrary, we are the busiest people of all times. Today social media has created addictive avenues of idle entertainment that are engulfing all of us. The same technologies that were expected to empower us, are enslaving us and making us dumber every day. While our cellphones, powered by artificial intelligence, are getting smarter, we are slowly losing our natural intelligence unknowingly.

Satvik, Sandeep and Ashok are three college friends meeting in Goa after a 25-year gap. While reminiscing about their college days, they discuss the craze of social media these days. They chance upon an idea of creating 'Paybook' – a new social media app that pays the users for their engagements. The app becomes an instant hit. This, however, also unfolds a series of events that take the friends to the unchartered territories.

This is not an anti-technology book because we can't go back to the caves. The objective of the book is to examine our infatuation with technology in personal lives and reset the counter in our favor.

The story aims to find the phone-life balance.

Contents

Contents

The Goa Meet

"We do not have Wi-Fi, talk to each other. Pretend it is 1995."

This was a funny signboard that Satvik noticed in Om Cafe, an upscale coffee shop on the Baga beach in Goa.

The cafe was set up in antique design, giving it an impression of medieval times. The dark wooden chairs appeared to be a great piece of workmanship. There were lanterns hanging at different places. Even the mechanical clock on the wall looked a century old. The most recent item probably was a sketch from the R K Narayanan's book *Malgudi Days*. This cafe was remarkably different from the rest on the beach. It was very much like experiencing a time machine for those who loved the simplicity of the pre-internet era.

The café was playing *"Tere Jaisa Yaar Kahan, Kahan aisa yarana"* (where will I find a friend like you, where will I find this friendship) a nice melodious Hindi song from Amitabh Bachchan's movie. It reminded Satvik and two of his accompanying friends of their youthful days.

"If nothing else we should spend some time in this café to listen to the song that it is playing," humming the song along, Satvik told his friends Sandeep and Ashok. The three friends used to sing this song quite often in college parties.

"Can you really believe it guys? They are trying to save the cost of the Wi-Fi," Satvik said.

Sandeep replied, "Satvik, it is not about cost saving, I went to one restaurant in Mumbai with a weird notice board at their entrance."

'Beware, you are entering the 'internet free' zone, your mobile phones will not work beyond this point, we have deployed jammers for your mobile phones. Don't be anxious, you will be fine. Just relax and enjoy your experience here."

"Most people will get stressed even at a notice like that, being offline even for a few moments can be scary. On the other hand, it can also be a luxury these days. I do see a rise in anti-internet rhetoric from last few years. I saw a holiday package that said, *'we offer internet-sabbatical to make you completely de-stressed and relaxed'*. Looks like people are getting crazy with their gadgets," Satvik said.

Sandeep replied, "I will tell you even a funnier story. Last week I went to a very upscale family restaurant. The ambience was amazing, they had created a garden-like setup with beautiful plants and flowers. There was a stream of water flowing down. It gave an impression of having dinner in a nice garden with small waterfalls. Then I noticed three people on the next table. They were all glued to their cellphones a few inches away from their faces. For the one hour that I was there, they hardly spoke a word, other than giving the order for the food. They did not even look at each other for the entire duration. Once the food was served, they switched the phone to one hand while the other hand grappled with the food to carefully navigate to their mouths without touching the screen on the other hand. One of them put a big piece of pickle in his mouth, thinking it was some vegetable. I wonder why they came to the restaurant. At one time, I thought I should take their picture and tweet – with a *'caption tag'* contest."

"For all you know they might be chatting with each other. I am not joking; I am telling you. For today's generation, it is easier to chat using emojis than trying to read actual emotions from real faces," Sandeep said.

"When Nokia launched their cell phone for the first time, their tagline was *'connecting people'*. That was a noble objective. Now, it has become connecting virtual people at the cost of real people," Ashok was a techno-skeptic. Even in this age of smartphones, he just carried a basic Nokia phone without any data network.

"The most precious thing today is to get undivided attention from the other person, the cellphones have taken away our ability to focus on the present moment," he added further.

"Even during the office meetings, I see many of our colleagues looking at their phones. This addiction is making us unproductive at all levels. I have given strict advice to my team members not to use their social media during office hours. But to tell you the fact, I myself find it very difficult to abide by the same. Once a junior team member sent me the screenshot of my Facebook post and the timestamp said it all. It revealed that I was browsing during our morning meeting – it was so embarrassing," Satvik added to the conversation.

"Satvik, you are so active on your Facebook. I saw you posting something or the other even today. You posted when you landed at the airport when we reached here at this beach and I am sure you would have posted the picture of this unique restaurant as well. It seems you believe that your followers must see everything that you experience real-time. You are broadcasting every moment of your life," Ashok was quick to interrupt him.

"Not only me but most of us have become like that today. You know, we sometimes joke in our house. The only way to get everyone in one place is to switch off the Wi-Fi router. Even my 10-year-old son runs up to the router connection point. Our dinner and lunch occasions have become somewhat like the scene you described from the restaurant," Satvik was embarrassed but candid in response.

Satvik, Ashok and Sandeep were meeting after 25 long years since they graduated from their engineering college. This meeting was in planning mode for several months. After a lot of deliberation, Goa was agreed as the reunion venue. They once again wanted to feel like those carefree days of early adulthood with full of energy and no worries and most importantly, plenty of time.

The year 1995 on café notice board had struck a chord with each of the three. It was the same year that they graduated from IIT Delhi, one of the most prestigious engineering college in India. The triad of Satvik, Ashok, and Sandeep was famous even during college times. They studied together, played together and were seen together most of the times in the hostel.

If there were any variations among them, it was in the exam scores. While Sandeep consistently scored good marks and topped in the class, Ashok barely managed to clear the exams. Satvik was not as good as Sandeep but a lot better than Ashok. It was a topic of common speculation about how the three friends produced different results for the same level of studies. Ashok had a simple explanation that it was more to do with the failure of the professors to get their teachings across different types of students. If Ashok failed in certain subjects, the responsibility squarely lied with the professors.

Engineering colleges are a great melting pot. Though these friends were from different cities and family backgrounds, their friendship did not discriminate each other. That is a good thing about four years of engineering kinship. It is a great leveler, students from different background blend homogenously to become best friends.

"Ok, let us pretend we are still in 1995," Satvik said and the three friends went inside the café.

The good thing about meeting college friends is that they can start their relationships from where they left 25 years ago. They can dip into the old times and feel nostalgic about every small thing they enjoyed during that time.

"We are the last descendants of internet free generations. We are the only set of people who have seen both the worlds - one when there were no cellphones and now when everyone has a smartphone. We were born into the first and grew into the other. It is amazing how technology has changed our lives in the last twenty-five years. We need to come to a place like this to feel unshackled. Our daily lives are nothing short of a mad rush. One thing that we all long for is real free time that we used to enjoy earlier," Sandeep said.

"Today we live in an age of 'technopoly' – our lives without cellphones are unimaginable, like fish without water, we can survive but very briefly," Satvik said.

Sandeep continued, "As a small child I could stare at the kites in the sky for hours. The kite fights used to be great fun. The clear blue sky was dotted with beautiful, multi-colored pieces of flying kites attached to strings. They came in different shapes, sizes and colors. Some of the kites would also have long tails wavering gently with wind flows. Their rise, high in the sky was a wonderful sight, like a giant bird dancing to our directions in the sky.

"Every evening, I would stand at the small window of my house and give fictitious identities to all the kites – good

5

kites, bad kites, rogue ones, lazy ones etc. They were all living beings for me, like my friends in the school. They looked the same but had different gaits. Some would circle around faster, some would be slow, some would swing on one side and some would go up like a rocket. I could easily map each of them to one of my friends in the class, I was myself one among them – high in the sky.

"Kite fighting was also the most enjoyable game for me. Even when I was not flying them, I was still somehow part of the game. Of the many kites in the sky, there would be one that would be 'my adopted kite'. For the next many hours that those kites would entangle with each other, I would pray for my kite to win the battle. I had no actual control over my adopted kite, I did not even know who was flying it, but still, I prayed for its success. Sometimes my wish came true, sometimes I was disappointed. However, it did not stop me from playing the same game the next day.

"The rule of the game was simple; the last standing kite would be the winner. Winning the kite fight was dependent on many factors like the agility of the kite, quality of *manja*, wind conditions, size of the spool and most importantly the skill of the person flying a kite. There were so many variables that the outcome was completely unpredictable and that added to the excitement of the game."

"The kite flying was not quite common in Mumbai, but we read great stories about them in the school textbooks," Satvik said, "As a child, I always wondered how a kite flew so smoothly in the sky."

Sandeep continued, "In my small town, it was one of the most popular sport. I used to have a wishful belief that when one of the kites would snap and fall, somehow it would land up in my balcony. I would imagine myself holding the string

6

and becoming a new proud owner of the beautiful kite. I was old enough to understand that the realistic possibility of the kite dropping exactly in my small balcony was almost zero, this, however, did not stop me from dreaming every day. I enjoyed playing this solitary game every day for hours, from the time the first kite that would appear in the sky to the last one that survived after the valiant fight or till it was very dark and I could not see the kites anymore.

"The world of kites was the dream world for me, something that people today will call virtual reality. I would get lost in that world weaving my own stories of victories and defeats," Sandeep went on the nostalgic trip.

"Have you visited your city recently? Have you noticed the change now?" Satvik asked.

"Yes, I keep visiting the place once a year to meet my parents. Every time I visit, I feel nostalgic, I feel a part of me in the city is lost. Last time when I visited, there were no more kites; the kids were more interested in playing video games," Sandeep replied.

"The new generation has progressed in many ways, after all no one flies a kite anymore these days. It has become a boring game. Instead, some of them play with drones with remote control. These high-tech drones today make the erstwhile kite look like a silly toy," Ashok said.

"Who would stare at the sky for hours looking at some random piece of papers loosely hung from a sagging string? It is too slow even to catch anyone's attention, forget staring at it for hours and weaving stories around each one of them. The kites are not exciting anymore. The kids today need something that is a lot faster, less physical but more direct and engaging. The brains of our kids have changed already. Their likes and dislikes have changed, most importantly everything has become fast and the attention span has reduced," Satvik tried to explain.

"Some of these skills will disappear with our generation, just like our caveman forefathers had excellent skills in tool making but today we have no clue about it," Sandeep added.

"That is called Darwin's law of natural selection. We learn new skills that we need during our times and forget the ones that we no longer use," Satvik said as a matter of fact.

The waiter walked up to the table by this time, asking for the order.

"Do you have a menu card?" Sandeep asked.

The waiter put up a tablet in front of them and requested them to choose.

"But in 1995 there were no tablets," Sandeep said jokingly. He placed an order for 2 mocha and one latte without sugar.

"You know Sandy, many of these technological innovations are like toothpaste. Once you have pressed it out of the tube, you can't put it back. It does not have a put-back button. Even with the right intent, this café can't operate without the new age digital devices," Satvik said.

"I recall reading somewhere – there have been few surveys asking people what they would like to lose in case they are accosted by a robber – their wallet or cellphone?" replied Ashok.

"And overwhelming majority respond – wallet, right?"

"That is still alright. I read about a survey in 2011, where youngsters had to choose from a list of things including cosmetics, their car, their passport, their phone and their sense of smell. They could retain only two from the list," said Sandeep.

"Don't tell me they chose to lose their sense of smell," Ashok laughed.

"Actually yes, 53% of those aged 16-22 years and 48% of those aged 23-30 years would prefer to give up their sense of smell if it meant they could keep their cellphones," replied Sandeep.

"You have all become digital prisoners, the cellphones control your lives. You can't live without them anymore," Ashok replied.

"Well Ashok, you can say that with your Nokia 3210," said Satvik.

"Don't make fun of this, I have read that now many people are lining up for this old model and Nokia has refurbished it into a new model," Ashok flashed his phone.

"You can also use this as a stone if some robber attacks you at night," Sandeep tried to pull his leg.

"Coming back to childhood games, I recall our days as kids. Cricket used to be the sensation. Almost every other child wanted to be a Kapil Dev or a Sunil Gavaskar. I recall the frenzy when India won the first cricket world cup. Our small playground was full of cricket enthusiasts, some with makeshift wickets made up of bricks and stones. At one point, I almost convinced my parents that cricket was the only possible profession for me," Satvik was fondly lost in his memories.

"There were more kids who actually played in the playground those days. We spent the whole day playing the game, especially during the holidays, nothing could match the fun ever. Our parents used to shout at us for not staying in the house, these days parents scold their kids for not going out in the field."

"There was no dearth of open space those days, today we hardly have open space other than some school playgrounds," replied Satvik.

"These days also kids play cricket, but in their mobiles phones. When I go to drop my son at the bus stand in the morning, I see several kids playing the game while waiting."

"Kids follow what they see in their parents and other adults. Today at any public space, you see everyone staring at their mobile phones. All of us are so engrossed with it that we almost forget to notice things around us," Ashok never liked the idea of smartphones since the beginning.

The waiter came back with coffee by this time and promptly kept the three white porcelain cups on the table.

"Do you want anything else, Sir?" the waiter asked.

"No thanks and we would call you in case we need anything," Ashok replied politely.

"See, I tell you, though they have put a catchy signboard at the gate encouraging people to talk, they would not want us here unless we keep ordering more stuff," Ashok looked at Sandeep and commented casually.

"You guys have made me wonder what kind of games I played as a kid. I had almost forgotten about them. I come from a small village near Guntur," Ashok said.

"Though we did not have a lot of awareness about the cricket nor we flew kites, our childhood was no less eventful.

"We had numerous games that people today would have even forgotten how to play.

"One fun game was - marbles. I can't tell you how much fun it used to be. Those small spherical pieces of glass with shiny eyes were the most precious possessions that we had

10

those days. There were different types of marble games, all of them required very different skills. The winner would keep accumulating the marbles if he could correctly hit another marble from a distance. It required tremendous concentration to cleanly hit a marble and win.

"And there was no dearth of improvised games like tops, gilli-danda and what not. Sometimes we played these games the whole day without getting tired. Those games are lost today and so is the fun associated with them," Ashok went on to describe the game.

"Not only the game is lost, these days you would hardly find any kid in the village. Villages have completely changed today, more than the cities of 80s. Although there are much better roads and electricity in each house, that way of life is lost.

"It is ironical that now that the roads have reached our villages, people have already left for cities. Today you will hardly find anyone other than a few old people in my village."

They were all feeling lost in the nostalgic good old days as kids. The coffee was over, the waiter came to the table promptly, "Do you want something else, sir?"

This was a signal for the friends to vacate the 1995 café seat in case they were not going to place another order.

"Let us go for a walk on the beach."

It was a pleasant evening. The gentle breeze alongside waves made the beach setting so calm and relaxed.

Incidentally, some kids were flying kites against the sea winds. These were not exactly the kind of kites that Sandeep was describing but still close.

Some distance away, a few kids were playing with a cricket bat and ball.

11

Another set of kids were playing with the sea pebbles, which remotely seemed like the game that Ashok was describing. The touch of cool sand on the bare legs was as refreshing as the sound of the sea waves. It was a wonderful experience.

They kept on walking, lost in thought of their childhood. It was late evening now slowly turning into night. The sight of the beautiful sunset made everyone busy as they wanted to take the perfect selfie with the red sun. A young couple was particularly interested in a picture where both would appear holding the setting sun on their palms together.

Slowly the sun set in the sea, but the absence of daylight did not change the festive mood at the Baga beach in any way. The mix of the crowd changed though. The family crowd thinned and finally disappeared. This was taken over by the young revelers dancing and enjoying to the loud music at multiple beach-side open bars. At night the beach turned even more colorful, just like a Diwali night in the city. The white waves of sea tides were faintly visible. They were accompanied by a low hissing noise.

While the beachside was well lit, the seaside was pitch dark except the blinkering lights of some far-off ships. There were some hawkers selling glowing multicolored hand bangles. Some were selling sharp laser lights that could be projected for a very long distance. Kids were having a good time playing with the laser lights and at times projecting on unsuspecting people.

The night at the beach was all about light, music and dance. As they walked across the beach, the blaring fusion of music from different bars created a unique festive atmosphere by themselves. At the entrance of each restaurant, the small oil lamps kept on tables appeared to provide more wonderful experience than the five-star candlelit dinners.

There were some lifeguards walking around. Satvik stopped one of them.

"Who would come to take a bath in the sea now, it is already night?"

"We have a lot of accidents at night, sir, some of these revelers get drunk and try to come near the sea waves. It is quite dangerous at night, but people don't realize that," replied the lifeguard.

"Is it safe to walk on the shore, we are not drunk, you see?"

"As long as you don't get close to water, it should be fine. Still, I would recommend that don't be here after 9 pm, it gets unsafe after that; not because of sea waves but because of petty crimes. Even the police stops patrolling after that time," responded the lifeguard.

"Let us do a Facebook live. I want other friends to enjoy this amazing view," said Satvik. He usually made it a point to capture the important moments on Facebook.

"Satvik, you are quite obsessed with sharing things on Facebook even at the cost of missing out the enjoyment of the present moment," said Sandeep.

"And once you post, I am sure you will keep checking for next few hours the reactions on your post. So, you will eventually miss out yourself what you want your friends to enjoy on Facebook," replied Ashok.

"In today's time of social media selfies, it appears what matters is not how much fun you are having but making sure that others know that you are having a good time. Broadcast is important – an event which is not publicized is a non-event," elaborated Sandeep with a sarcastic look towards Satvik.

13

The walk on the sea beach at night was so enjoyable that the three friends did not stop even after the warning of the lifeguard. Now they reached a secluded end that was completely deserted.

"Let us return now, it is already dark," Sandeep said.

Satvik spotted a small fire lit behind an abandoned boat. It appeared like a fishing boat.

"Let us go there," Satvik said.

"Who would light a fire in this secluded place?" he was curious to know and goaded the other two friends to walk up to the place.

When they reached nearby, they saw one person with disheveled hair and long beard sitting by the fire. He was arranging the pieces of wood to light properly. He seemed oblivious to the presence of the three friends.

"Look at the thing in his hand – it looks like ganja; he seems to be one of those addicts who are caught at the Goa beaches many times. Let us get back to our place, it may not be safe here," Ashok said.

Though Ashok said it in a hushed tone, the person on the beach heard it. Without waiting for an introduction, he said, "You are right in saying that I have a piece of ganja in my hand. It is illegal to have it on the main beach; hence I have to come this far.

"However, don't think that what you all have in your hand is any better."

"What do you mean?" Satvik asked.

"The cellphone that all of you carry is a bigger drug than this cannabis. And you all are addicted to it. I can still live without ganja for days but none of you can live without your phones even for a few days.

Moreover, when I take ganja, I am aware that I am doing something illegal. I try to control it to minimize the damage. On the contrary, you are not even aware that you are getting addicted to something that is far more harmful."

"This is an atrocious comparison, we use our cells to connect with our near and dear ones, play music, learn things and do our chores like paying bills etc. It has made our lives easy and given us free time," Satvik countered.

"And what do you do with that free time?" said the man.

"Most of you would check what your friends are updating on Facebook or Twitter or some news or whatever? In fact, you have no free time, because every pause in your daily routine is used for going through the mindless updates and news, which essentially has no real significance. The free time that you get, you use it to forget yourself even more. This is what my ganja also does.

The phone that you claim connects you to the world actually cuts your own link with yourself, it makes you a loner."

"It is our choice, we use it to amplify our potential," Satvik replied.

"Think again, it is no longer a choice, you are all dependent on them more than my dependence on these weeds," the man replied.

"If there is one thing that has deprived you all from happiness the most, it is this mobile phone. Throw it in these waves and you would all discover yourself."

With this, the man threw his small hookah far in the rising waves, "Can you all throw your cells just like this?"

The three friends hurriedly returned without saying anything more to the man. It was not safe, what if the man attacked them with a knife or robbed them. They got scared, but there was some mystic truth in what he said in the state of rage.

Our Digital World

Next day the three friends went to the beach early in the morning. Swimming in the sea waves was one of the topmost things in the plan. There were few people around, playing with the waves. Every time the high tide came with full force, they held their hands together and jumped in a synchronized way to avoid getting fully submerged. When the waves returned, it sweeped in the sand along with it, giving a feeling that the land under the feet was slipping. The three friends played with waves for long.

After a few hours of fun and frolic, fully exhausted, they came out of the water and walked up to the beach. Now it was a strong sun. There were few beach umbrellas that some restaurant owners had set up as an extended catchment area.

"How much do you charge for these umbrellas?"

"200 rupees for every hour sir, you can also order food and drinks."

"Ok, we will rent this for 2 hours, meanwhile get us three coke and some French fries," said Satvik.

"For us, this sun is too strong but look at those foreigners enjoying the sunbath," Ashok pointed towards a group of tourists relaxing.

"You know a joke about Goa? I heard it somewhere that foreigners come to Goa to see Indians and Indians go to Goa to see the foreigners," Satvik said as the three friends laughed.

"These days you see relatively fewer foreigners here, in fact, you may see more Indians in the streets of London than westerners on Goa beaches."

"The reason is not that the foreigners have stopped visiting, instead more Indians from other states come to Goa compared to ten years back, so the foreigners get outnumbered. By the way, now Indians no longer come to Goa to see foreigners, they come here for the cheap booze," replied Ashok.

"And also, to upload some nice pictures on Facebook," added Satvik.

While the three friends were enjoying the day, the discussion of the previous night with the man on the beach was still resonating in their mind.

"Was the person right that we are all addicted to our phones, and it is more dangerous than his hookah?"

"He was fear-mongering. The technology always evolves, and we need not be fearful about it. Rather we all must be in sync with the times that we live in. There have been technology naysayers who predicted doomsday with every new thing. Do you remember the Yahoo chat?" Satvik asked.

"Yes, very much," Ashok replied.

"The internet cafes used to be full of people who would chat for the whole day. They would even skip their lunch. Some of us even used to bunk our classes to go to the nearby internet cafes," Satvik recalled.

"There used to be anonymous chat rooms. Many of us, as first-time users would spend the whole day talking to strangers," added Ashok.

"It was a bigger addiction than Facebook is today. It was the first time that most of us got a taste of anonymity while interacting with real people. A lot of fake love stories also got created during these chats," Satvik giggled.

"Yes, anonymity does funny things at times. Sometimes two boys apparently would fall in love with each other during such chats assuming the other person was a girl. We used to play pranks with unsuspecting friends," replied Sandeep.

"asl? (Age, Sex, Location?) I still recall the first question people used to ask in those rooms."

"And invariably all the boys of our age would try to be as creative in responding to the same. I used to chat as Sonam, age 24 from Delhi. It used to be great fun," Sandeep replied.

"And Yahoo chat rooms are dead already. My ten-year-old son would even laugh at an idea like that today. Yahoo that brought that revolutionary concept as a company is struggling to survive now," replied Satvik.

"Chat room as a concept died as fast as it got popularized. There were also some photo sharing sites those days like Myspace, Orkut etc. – all are extinct now. That was the first wave of social media," Sandeep said.

"Our parents those days said that internet addiction was the worst thing that could happen to young minds. But look where we are today," Satvik explained.

"We have moved from 'internet cafes' to 'internet-free cafes' as the new trend. All these fancy things go through a full cycle."

"Ten years down the line will Facebook also become extinct like the Orkut of last decade?" Ashok asked.

"We don't know, the future is more uncertain today than it was ten years ago. But if you observe carefully none of those things died till something more interesting came up. The death of the first wave of social media gave rise to Facebook and Twitter," Satvik tried to explain.

"Facebook derives its popularity from a more fundamental vulnerability of the human mind – the need to get continuous social endorsements," Sandeep added.

"You mean to say Facebook is exploiting the bug of our evolutionary brain?" asked Ashok.

"Kind of yes. Unlike Yahoo chats, Facebook banks on the need of our mind to get constant social approvals. We look outside for the re-affirmation of our well-being. The 'likes' and 'positive comments' provide similar kicks as real-life achievements. Now there are scientific pieces of evidence that Facebook engagements release dopamine - a neurotransmitter responsible for the sensation of pleasure like winning a race and qualifying in an exam," Sandeep replied.

"Don't tell me Mark Zuckerberg studied neuroscience before creating this product," Satvik asked.

"I think it could have been an accidental discovery when he launched this networking site amongst the Harvard students. But something in it was damn right that clicked so well that it has spread like wildfire today even at the cost of privacy," Sandeep replied.

"Yes, that is true. Noted futurist Kevin Kelly, in his book 'The Inevitable', says that we are willing to provide incredible details about ourselves in return for social validation. This essentially means that vanity trumps privacy when it comes to choosing between the two. This insight is at the root of the business model of Facebook. It provides people with social validation in return for sharing personal data," Satvik added.

"It is strange how people change their behavior with time. Do you recall, we all used to have personal albums with family photos? They used to be the most private possessions of the families. Only very close friends and family members had access to the albums. They had imprinted memories of all times, good and bad," Ashok asked.

"Could you have ever imagined our grandfathers sharing those intimate albums publicly with strangers they hardly knew?" Ashok added further with surprise.

"It would have appeared as weird as pasting our personal diaries on the roadside lamp posts. What could be the point of sharing personal photos with little known or random people?"

"Today, with Facebook, we invariably share our photographs and sometimes very intimate experiences with practically so many people we hardly know. Our family album is on display and we have no qualms about it. We feel happy about the likes and the comments we get. We feel more comfortable broadcasting our moments than preserving them," Sandeep replied.

"Today, we are living in a shared experience economy – our lives are networked, and it is a really good thing. An experience not shared is as bad as wasted, we are becoming more open and liberal," Satvik explained that this is actually a progressive human behavior than our secretive past.

"But what about privacy, our fundamental human right?" asked Ashok.

"Privacy is wishful thinking. If we can derive happiness by sharing experiences with others, why be diffident about it. I know some of my friends who run a marathon only to share that on their Facebook wall. At the end of the day, it improves their health and motivates others to do the same. When people boast of their achievements, it also encourages others to strive harder and do better," Satvik elaborated.

"While Facebook provides a sense of achievement, most often, it is also the cause of numerous cases of depression and other mental health issues," Sandeep said.

"This is all hogwash that Facebook is creating mental health issues as if these mental problems never existed before in our society. People have been getting depressed for a thousand other reasons since ages. Why blame Facebook for that. If anything, it helps people by making more friends and interacting with the world that otherwise is impossible," Satvik responded.

"Ok, Satvik tell me, how many friends you have on Facebook?" asked Ashok.

"2522 friends."

"And how many of them you actually know," asked Ashok.

"It does not matter, but they have chosen to share their lives with me just as I do with them and collectively it has made us all happier," Satvik defended his huge friend list.

"It will be a stretch to call Facebook connection as a friend; you can call them light acquaintances. Numerous researches show that they do not make you happier in general. It is better to have a handful of deep friendships rather than having hundreds of acquaintances," Sandeep responded.

"Something that people call 3 AM friends? Certainly, you don't search for them on Facebook," replied Satvik.

"Right, when one browses through the variety of contents from all kinds of people, it creates a sense of emptiness and a feeling that other's lives are more eventful. It is vanity at display," Ashok had always been less optimistic about Facebook.

"Facebook is unhappiness bundled as happiness – it is essentially a fake book. At Facebook, we are all alone together.

Though I have a Facebook account, I use it very sparingly," Sandeep spoke like a psychologist this time.

"Facebook can be addictive; I know even my teenager niece is so hooked to it that it is tough for us to extricate her. It has affected her attention and studies. It is particularly bad for an impressionable mind," Ashok said.

"Not only kids, but even the grown-ups like us are also affected badly. Looking at the holiday pictures of her friends, my wife always believes that we have a boring life. This sometimes becomes a reason for fights among us," Sandeep added.

"According to psychologists and family counselors, some of these couples who post such adorable anniversary pictures on Facebook and get hundreds of likes, in reality, have very bitter relations," he added further.

"Make no mistake, Facebook is making us all fake. We have split personalities - one that we share on our Facebook profile pretending to have a great happy-go-lucky life and the other one which is real, a boring self. For as much as we gloat about the selective moments of happiness that we share, we ardently guard that our real life does not get revealed," replied Ashok.

"Not only that, but today the social media is also destroying relationships," Ashok added.

"I think it will be foolish to conclude that social media will vanish one day. Maybe Facebook may not exist, but the inherent need of social tool will always be there. Any new technology, in general, is looked at with suspicion that it will impact the human mind negatively," replied Satvik.

"Let me explain why I say that. This was the same case when writing was invented. Before that, there was only oral tradition of communication. People believed that writing brings down the brain's wholesome experience to learn by watching, talking and hearing. The same fear was expressed when the telephone was invented. Some people believed that this would impair their skill of face to face communication. Years down the line, now we know that none of them happened. In fact, some communication can happen more effectively in writing or on-call rather than face to face talk. We eventually evolve and feel more empowered by every new technological adoption," Satvik explained further.

"It is because of tools like Facebook that we have so many friends and we are able to communicate with so many of them. It is a non-intrusive communication mechanism of being social," Satvik added more insights on the advantages of Facebook. He was all praise for a tool like Facebook. He never understood the skepticism that Ashok and Sandeep had, especially Sandeep because he was a tech wizard and a PhD in communication technology.

"I think you guys are getting old like our grandparents always used to tell stories about how things were so cheap during their times - they had dinner in one rupee that can't even fetch a cup of tea today. They, however, omit the fact that most of them hardly earned more than a few hundred rupees in the entire month. So, if you take the proportion of earnings to the price of goods, we have progressed several times, but the folklores continue," Satvik said sarcastically.

"Satvik, do you really believe that social media like Facebook do not harm the users?" Ashok asked Satvik one more time.

"Like all new technologies, there is a utopian view and a dystopian view. But it looks like you are not convinced that people can use Facebook effectively. That's why you don't even have a Facebook account. For every new tool, there is some learning involved in how to use it effectively. But you eventually get over it if you start using. I was suffering from the initial anxiety sometime back – constant checking of my Facebook app so that I don't miss anything. I would scroll through several times, only to feel exhausted and tired about the same," Satvik said.

"That is called FOMO – fear of missing out, in Psychology. This eventually creates stress in you and can also make you depressed. If you have a frequent (hourly urge) to check your social media account, you might well be suffering from it," Sandeep replied.

"Yes, correct. But that was my inability to handle it. I was not able to control my urge; social media need not be blamed for that. You can equally have the urge for eating sugar every hour."

"If I ever need to slow down, I can set a time limit on the app. Alternatively, I can just delete the app from my phone or in the worst case can de-activate my account. It's we who are defining our relationship with the social media and not the other way around. Moreover, Facebook can still thrive despite some people like you guys criticizing it," replied Satvik.

Both Ashok and Sandeep knew that Satvik was riding a vehicle which he thought he was in control of while he was addicted to it. Satvik was like a celebrity on Facebook. All his posts eventually get hundreds of likes. While Ashok hated all kind of social media and considered it as an evil, Satvik was on the other extreme of the scale. Sandeep was probably somewhere in-between.

"Right, technological innovation does not require our permissions, they need our forgiveness. I am not surprised how different social media platforms are evolving with their own distinct characteristics," Sandeep replied.

"And they are all bad in their own rights. If Facebook is a medium of vanity, twitter is a medium of outrage. If you look at the trending topics on twitter, you will realize that everybody in this world is angry with something or the other. There are thousands of tweets on any topic and almost everyone takes a radical position with the 140 characters expression," Ashok said.

"I am quite active on twitter. My PhD guide says that twitter is more effective in building your personal brand and shaping public opinions," replied Sandeep.

"Ashok, I think you are being too critical of twitter as well. You are a social media ignoramus, but you are already in the minority in today's time," Satvik countered Ashok's arguments once again.

"According to me, twitter is the most empowering tool. Earlier when I did not like a newspaper article, the only option that I had was to write a letter to the editor which could have been thrown in the dustbin. Even when the editor received the letter, he had the absolute privilege to publish it or just ignore it. Twitter has given me the power that I can immediately react to it publicly. I tell you all these mainstream media – all of them have their own agenda, they are not neutral. Twitter gives us a mechanism to get even with them. Twitter is people's voice against the large establishments. In today's world, social media is the real check and balance," Satvik explained to Ashok and Sandeep.

"But how do you make out the correct information from the fake ones? Twitter trends can be sponsored, there are thousands of people giving an opinion about everything?" Ashok asked.

"When you check twitter, you understand there can be fake news, there is no façade about that. The onus of finding the right news from the wrong ones is on you. If you are so particular, you can still rely on the verified accounts of media channels and journalists. That option of old-world communication is still with you. But my personal experience has been that most of the times common twitter handles provide more authentic and unbiased information than the verified handles," Satvik replied.

"I do admit that sometimes I used to get hooked on to twitter trends and hashtags. Some of them got me so addicted that I would keep following it up for hours – just to see what people are talking about, even when I was hardly connected with the event or the cause," Sandeep added.

"That is called idle entertainment – some bit of it is not bad but do keep a check when you are spending long hours just checking the hashtags," Satvik replied.

"Remember, Twitter, like any communication medium, is just a platform, it is not good or bad per se. However, the way one uses it can make it look good or bad – an empowering tool or an addictive outrage manufacturer."

"These social media platforms will eventually die; people will get bored of it. Moreover, future generations may not have enough time to waste on useless tweets and Facebook posts, they will have other meaningful things to do. Already teens in the US and UK are leaving Facebook because they don't find it cool anymore," Ashok said.

"You are wrong Ashok, with the advancement in technology we will have more and more free time that we won't know what to do with. Just think about it, at one point in time everyone was engaged in agriculture but today only a minuscule percentage of population work in fields. Most of us today work in manufacturing or service industries. Now, these works will also increasingly get replaced with automation robots and artificial intelligence. We will have more output, higher productivity but a lot of free time to spare," replied Satvik.

"The technology will make our lives so comfortable that we will have abundant food, water, energy and other resources. With the advancement in medical facilities, we would live far longer than our earlier generations. This will eventually create problems for society – how to meaningfully engage people in purposeful work. Many countries are already experimenting with the ideas of Universal Basic Income," replied Sandeep as he was most abreast with the latest technological advancements.

"It was easier to keep poor people happy by providing them with food and some basic amenities. But how can one keep an overpaid engineer happy, who already has all basic amenities but is just bored with things? There are more people depressed today than there are hungry people. Humanity is moving towards the abundance, but the prolonged pleasure brings in a terrible problem – boredom and rise of a useless class that is not only unemployed but also unemployable. With increasing wealth, more people are confused about the larger purpose in lives – the social media is like a virtual reality that provides them with a detour. So, in the near future, even the governments would want us to be on Facebook and they may even pay us for that," Satvik tried to convince Ashok as well.

"Possible, today I read in the newspaper that according to a study, a typical Facebook user would demand more than 70,000 rupees per year to deactivate his or her account," said Sandeep.

"That way I am already a millionaire as I am not using Facebook at all," Ashok countered.

"I am not joking, it was an experiment conducted in the US among two sets of college students, a community and an online sample.

"Winners were paid on the proof that their Facebook account was deactivated for a certain time. Since it was a real experiment with financial outcome, people could bid for the same. The outcome was that the students placed higher value than the community members. A few participants refused to bid at all, thinking that it was not a welcome possibility. Don't forget that many people also run their businesses on Facebook," Sandeep explained.

"Since Facebook has 2.2 billion users, that way, they have already created worth more than 2 trillion dollars. Their current market valuation is far lesser though," said Satvik.

"The way I see it if the users are willing to spend several hours on the site per day, there is no doubt that they must be deriving some value out of it. I am thinking of an idea to capitalize on this trend," Satvik added.

"Not really, social media, in general, has changed the way of our life but there is no evidence that it has made us richer or more productive at work in any way. If anything, it has made us dumber and more inattentive in our real-life affairs," Ashok did not buy their argument and compulsive justification of social media in everyone's lives.

"A few days back, I read a report that a person committed suicide while on Facebook live and many people watched that online. The exhibitionism has grown to a dangerous level already," Ashok added.

"People do not commit suicide because of Facebook. In fact, the social media company is creating an early warning system that can alert police in case their algorithm finds something wrong. I heard Facebook is ranking all its users on such mental health symptoms using its artificial intelligence," Sandeep explained Ashok.

"But isn't it scary that a private company has such private data about everyone. That is why my party has been demanding a ban on all these foreign social media companies. It can be against the national security," replied Ashok.

Satvik knew that it was pointless to argue with Ashok on this topic beyond a point. However, it was important to convince him to come on-board with the idea that he was pondering about. After all, Ashok was resourceful, thanks to his active political life. While Satvik had a star-like following in the virtual world, Ashok had real life following from numerous people. His fiery speeches had won him a very prominent place in his party.

A New Idea

The third day was put aside for casinos. They went for a trip on a floating casino which had an amazing ambience. The ship was pretty much like a grand hotel in the Mandovi River. While the window view was calm, the inner deck of the ship was full of festivities and noisy like a fish market. The multi-coloured blinking lights on the stalls were specially designed to catch everyone's attention. Most of the stalls were manned by the ladies in shiny dresses. They were explaining a variety of available gaming options like roulette, teen patti, blackjack, the usual slot machines and money reels.

"Goa is one of the rare places in India where gambling is legal," said Satvik.

"Many Indians come here precisely for this reason. Cheap alcohol and free gambling make it a heady combination. You can get drunk and lose all your money in this casino managed by these ladies. I remember how in our early college days we were desperate to visit such places, but it was a 'no-go zone' for us. We were always sent back for the proof of legal age," Ashok replied.

"And the government taxes this heavily to make money out of it. So, it is good for the local economy as well, win-win for everyone," said Sandeep.

"Sir, what drinks would you like?" the waiter asked.

"Get us three Kingfisher beer to start with," replied Satvik.

"I don't know any of these games to even try my luck," said Ashok.

"The rules in all these gambling games are pretty simple even for a layman. They are designed in such a way that it makes you believe that you can surely hit the jackpot, but the mathematical odds are always against it. Gambling is a psychological mind game in reality," Sandeep explained.

"I somehow find all these table dealers intimidating as if they are going to trick you into playing the game and steal your money. They are also dressed like magicians," said Ashok.

"Ok, let us try this wheel of fortune in that case. You just need to bet where the spinning wheel will finally stop with the position of the marker. It just cost 100 rupees for one bet," Satvik told Ashok.

The table was crowded already. Many people had selected their lucky numbers.

"2, 4 and 6 - small even numbers are my favorites," replied Ashok.

The casino dealer swung the giant wheel and it started rotating. Five more people joined with their bets when the lady said – "no more bets now."

The two minutes of wheel-spinning felt like a long time for Ashok. Finally, it stopped, and one of the pointed numbers was 4.

"You get 1000 rupees," said the lady who was spinning the wheel.

"I did not know, I was so good at random guessing," exclaimed Ashok.

"Many times, we are not aware of our hidden skills," smiled Satvik.

"See you were so critical of gambling, now that you have won you feel so happy. This is called beginner's luck – the first time you play a game, you always win," replied Sandeep.

Satvik and Sandeep tried next and both lost five thousand rupees each.

"So, from the three of us today, the casino has gained nine thousand rupees. But you know the strange thing?"

"We will all talk about how Ashok won ten times than each of us losing five times that amount. If three of us were to post our day on Facebook, Ashok would happily post his win while two of us would never post about our losses," said Sandeep.

"And all our friends who check Facebook would believe how the wheel of fortune is a fantastic game to make money. This is how partial truth spreads on social media. Thank god, I am still not part of this fake world," said Ashok.

"No one wants to talk about losing, right? We all want to pretend that we are the winners. Our mind learns to even package our failure as success when it comes to sharing with others," Sandeep replied.

"Please don't start your lecture on human psychology again."

"Let him explain that Ashok, he is absolutely right. In fact, since last few days I got the inspiration to do something riding on the current craze of social media," Satvik explained.

"Getting a business idea in a casino after a few bottles of beer? Isn't it too risky?" asked Ashok.

"I am serious. I think the time is right to create a new type of virtual casino that indirectly exploits this human psychology – something super exciting in this social media age. The old-style casinos have become outdated just like kite flying games of our childhood," said Satvik.

"There are already so many online gambling sites on social media, and people get defrauded every day. The government should come down heavily on them and shut them down," Ashok responded.

"Satvik has a point Ashok. See, you can say whatever, but the social media age is here to stay, it is an irreversible process. People will use more and more of Facebook, even if some of us fret about it occasionally," Sandeep said.

"Fully agree, Sandy. Actually, I am working on an idea leveraging this increasing trend of social media. We would introduce it as the next wave of social engagement," said Satvik.

"What exactly do you mean?" Ashok asked.

"See Facebook was the idea of the last decade, it has an inherent flaw in its business model, and hence it would eventually get superseded like the Orkut of the past," Satvik explained further.

"What does that mean, if people are going to adopt more of social media, how can Facebook lose out?" Ashok asked.

"Because people will soon realize that Facebook is making a fool of them," replied Satvik.

"You are talking in riddles, explain it for laymen like us," said Ashok.

"See, Facebook is the only platform where the post creator does not get any reward for writing which in a way is the writer's intellectual property. If you write a newspaper article, you will get paid for it, but if the same article you write on Facebook, you will not get paid a penny even if you get thousands of likes. However, do keep in mind that Facebook makes money eventually due to these interactions of people," replied Satvik.

"That is true because, for people, Facebook is not for earning but more for connection and fun. They say Facebook is free," Ashok said.

"Never believe any promotional mumbo-jumbo if they say that their product is free for you. Only, in that case, the product is you. In fact, Facebook earns money due to its unsuspecting users. Always remember that the free things are most expensive, there are no free lunches ever," replied Sandeep.

"Think of it like this – an average person spends 30 minutes every day on Facebook, he or she takes out this time from his productive work hours. Why can't this be converted into fun plus earning time?" Satvik explained further.

"How can people earn money while browsing through Facebook?" Ashok asked.

"How about creating a new social media app where people will get paid for creating posts that have a large number of likes and comments?" Satvik had thought through this idea in detail.

"And who will pay those post creators?" Sandeep asked.

"This is the most important part so let me explain-

Let us treat Facebook as a market where some people sell creativity and fun (those who create engaging posts), and other people buy (those who react) them. Those who consume entertainment and fun, pay for the same. This is what you do when you go to watch a movie or a play.

This is how all platform companies and intermediaries like banks work. In layman's term, they take money from one set of people to lend to another set of people at a higher rate. The time has come to try something similar in social media as well.

Think of Amazon – how do they make money? They only provide a platform for the buyers and the sellers to interact. They carve out their share from the trade margin of the buyer and sellers. Their key advantage is that they control the interaction point between the buyers and sellers. They capture the entire data and understand the e-commerce pattern. This data eventually generates money for them.

Also, don't forget that digital advertisers pay Facebook as well, and that is the primary source of revenue for Facebook.

So, we will have multiple ways to make money – through the advertisers, acquiring the data and acting as an intermediary between content creators and consumers," explained Satvik.

"This sounds interesting, but Facebook has already exploited all that and they have a formidable presence. There is no competitor even close to them," said Ashok.

"We will create a new social media sensation. We will name it Paybook."

"The users of Paybook can earn money by investing their time on social media – more the engagements, more the earnings. Just like this giant casino, we will create a busy marketplace where money will change hands during 'like' of any post. We will be like a bank for the newest invention of this decade - social media currency."

"But who will set up this marketplace – banks get their money from RBI. We will all go broke if we start paying everyone," replied Ashok.

"We will be like RBI, but instead of giving real money, we will deal with Paybook points. Just like shops provide loyalty points for every shopping, we will provide Paybook points to the users that can be converted to real rewards based on our terms and conditions," replied Satvik.

"The Paybook points can be exchanged between the post creator and consumers. We can write an algorithm that can make sure that people who participate the most gain the most. I am confident that Sandeep with his PhD in information technology can easily write one," Satvik added further.

"What if everyone starts creating random posts and starts flooding the timelines and pages?" Ashok was not confident of the idea, it looked so lame and straightforward.

"All those things can be controlled by creating rules in the platform – for example, if many posts from an individual do not generate enough engagement, their Paybook points can be curtailed. We can always write artificial intelligence tools to make sure that everyone contributes productively and those who create maximum positive engagements get paid the most," Satvik shared the insights from what looked like a well thought through plan.

"In the digital world, it is called gamification. For this to work, we need three elements – a broad structure (rules of engagement), freedom to act (respond to posts) and finally a reward system (positive or negative reinforcements) to evaluate. Our minds can get hooked onto any game that has these three elements crafted well. It does not matter even if there are no real rewards and they are virtual numbers like the loyalty points," replied Sandeep.

"See friends, Paybook will earn money only because of its participants and hence it is only fair to share the rewards whether real or virtual with those members who enrich the platform for the advertisers," Satvik seemed to agree with Sandeep.

"People are already addicted to Facebook without even getting paid, what will happen if Paybook starts generating money for them, however small it may be. In a country like India, where there is huge unemployment, every poor person will treat this as a money-making business," Ashok said. He suddenly thought of hundreds of unemployed people in his village.

"Not only poor and unemployed, but even the rich people would also use this opportunity more to show off and vanity. Many of them will be willing to pay for the same," Satvik said.

"Let me ask a simple question. What do poor people want?"

"Money," replied Ashok.

"And what do the rich people want?"

"Fame, social recognition?"

"And they wouldn't mind spending some of their money for the same."

"The real problem in society today is not the lack of wealth but its distribution. We are only setting up a wealth re-distribution platform and making everyone willing participants in the process. It is a demand-supply thing. Paybook will be a platform where people who have a lot of money can happily spend it to earn fame and social acceptance. The common people, on the other hand, will be equally happy to earn some change for providing their applause," explained Satvik.

"In today's time, a celebrity exists and earns money because of his or her fan base. I am sure he or she will not mind sharing some of the wealth to create an even wider fan base. You can also look at it from the angle of charity," Satvik added.

This interpretation was a revelation for Ashok. A few moments back, it appeared as an exploitative gambling idea, suddenly it looked like a much noble cause in line with his party ideology of reducing the inequality among people. But he was still not convinced if it could be that straightforward.

"Are you really serious, some people will pay just to show off on social media? It is like buying out applause and feeling happy about it. Do people have that much money?" Sandeep asked.

"In the book publishing business, there is a term called vanity publishing. In this kind of publishing the author pays the publisher to publish a book. He even pays the readers to read the book and post reviews. On the face of it, it appears only a fool will do it. But it is big business, and many celebrities and famous people happily do it. This is a form of advertising and is acceptable in other areas of art like movies, etc.," replied Satvik.

"See Sandy, today everyone wants to be famous. Once your basic needs are met, the Maslow's need hierarchy kicks in. There are only two ways to get famous – through your professional work or social recognition. The professional world is very cut and dry. It is like a steep pyramid – only one person in a company can be the CEO and rest all fall by the wayside. It leaves little opportunity to get fame beyond some fortunate people. People realize that, especially those who are in their mid-life conundrum. These people have disposable money to spend and they would not mind spending it on getting famous on social media.

"Even today, Facebook sponsorship works exactly like that. You can pay for a certain number of likes on your posts and Facebook will promote your post accordingly. People pay for the post likes, quite a few of them. Our job is to create an avenue for people who want to gain social fame. In today's time and age, it does not matter if it is a real accomplishment or some fake praise. If you see a post of your friend with five hundred like, you may almost fall for it, irrespective of what is written. This is the reason of craze behind the viral posts," Satvik replied.

"That seems really interesting - in economics we have studied about the poor common man and rich elites in society. They were never on the same platform or accessible to each other like social media today. The Marxist theory is primarily about the constant struggle of the proletariat against the elites. With the advent of the industrial revolution, there has been a rise of 'middle class' during the last few years. These middle-class people, over the world, have been most industrious and changed the societies," explained Ashok.

"Right, in broad terms we had three classes in society– rich class, poor class and middle class. But soon it is going to change. Thanks to automation, we will have far less work to do. In this age of social media, we will soon have a new class called 'useless class' – a growing bunch of well-to-do but bored people looking for some idle entertainment," Satvik explained.

"Ashok your communist theory will become irrelevant in this new social media age. The proletariat and egalitarians will never fight each other, rather both will be engrossed in the virtual reality games where physical wealth does not matter. There is no scope of Marxist revolution anymore," Sandeep sometimes enjoyed pulling Ashok's legs who often talked of the revolutions and class wars.

Social Currency

The last day of the trip was deliberately planned to be unplanned. The three friends hired three bikes and went around the place for the whole day. They ate in roadside shops, visited some ancient temples and churches on the way, finally to spend some time in a spice garden. After a long walk in the garden, they were offered Feni, a local Goan drink that Satvik was particularly looking forward to.

As they were sipping their drink, an American man in his early twenties was busy taking pictures of various plants and spices.

"Only in western countries, you see young people travelling abroad by themselves. For most of us, the early 20s was just about studies and preparing for jobs. Any adventures like were a taboo," observed Ashok.

"It has to do with rising economic standards, our kids will have more time to experiment with things like this hopefully. While many people do it out of genuine interest, quite a few people also do it to brag about it on Facebook," replied Sandeep.

"You have to study human psychology to understand it better. I have done some research on this. Have you heard of a term called 'fake-a-vacation'? Today there is a full industry that has evolved with social media," explained Satvik.

"As per one of the Times surveys, as much as 30% of Americans admitted to engaging in vacation doctoring, saying that they posted a photo on social media that makes it look like they are staying, eating or visiting somewhere more expensive than they actually were. For millennial, this ratio was 56%.

"There are many small companies that have packages for different holiday trips to places like Hawaii, Las Vegas or Disneyland that starts as low as 30 dollars. All you need to do is share some of your photos, and the company will doctor them to make it look like you have visited the place. This can give you the online bragging rights no lesser than the ones who have actually visited those places.

"And the sociologists say, after all, it is not such a bad thing. It helps an average American avoid going in debt ($1,100 as per the survey) while travelling," explained Satvik.

"This is really amusing, I never knew people could fake their vacation photos, and there is already a cottage industry of fake-a-vacation," replied Ashok.

"The popular saying has been 'Fake it till you make it'. Now it should be modified to 'Why make it when you can fake it'," replied Sandeep.

He added, "There was a much talked about story of a Dutch girl who posted about her travel to Phuket. She was seen sharing videos of eating local food, going to temples and shopping in market areas. It was super hit and she got a lot of followers. In the end, she divulged that it was all shot in her city in Amsterdam, many of the scenes being from her home itself after some fake setup. But she was able to fool even her friends and family members."

"All of us have a digital personality today that is more important than the real one. We all care for our virtual image on social media."

"Okay, let me ask you one basic thing, what is one thing that every human being wants today?" Satvik asked.

"Happiness?"

"Yes, and happiness is always elusive. That is why we keep chasing it, be it a holiday to a distant location or buying a car. There are tons of books written on the purpose of human life and happiness.

"But now there is a biological definition of happiness. Scientists have discovered that the incidents by themselves do not provide happiness, but it is our biochemical reaction to the events that gives us happiness. The specific actions of the neurons are rewarded by the flow of a neurotransmitter called Dopamine. This is how the brain learns a desirable behavior – more dopamine indicates it was a pleasurable experience and the brain strengthens that behavior. Less flow of dopamine indicates that the behavior need not be learnt. This is called reinforcement theory of brain learning.

"There was an experiment done in the monkeys to stimulate the part of the brain (by pulling a lever) that would electrically stimulate the part of the brain that releases dopamine. The monkeys eventually pulled the levers repeatedly to the extent of starving themselves. So, the flow of dopamine can even overcome the basic biological needs like hunger.

"Our brain does not know the external world; it only reacts to the flow of dopamine that makes us feel happy. So, if we can somehow control the flow of these hormones, we can achieve this evasive happiness without doing anything. Today some of these drugs are already being used for depression cases.

"The same dopamine is released when one sees his or her photographs being liked by many people on social media. So, it is possible to derive similar happiness in the virtual world that one can get from physical achievements, the mind does not differentiate. Hence vanity is not necessarily bad – it can really make you feel happy. We are only fulfilling a basic human need in the form of our Paybook app."

Satvik always gave a psychological and neurological explanation of why the Paybook app will be very popular among people.

"I know a little bit about the psychology of Indians. The moment we say that browsing and posting message will be a paid activity, there will be thousands of people who would come onboard to earn something. Soon they will discover that we have no money to pay them and they will come baying for our blood. Have you seen when some of these chit-fund guys get caught by the mob?" Ashok said.

"That's right, even if we get some celebrities or rich people who can indirectly sponsor and promote their posts, they will not be the first people to come on our platform. They will wait for the masses to join our app first. The common people will join only if they get the money first. We will have a cash flow issue to start with. We will have more people demanding money than the ones sponsoring. We will go broke as soon as we start," Sandeep replied.

"I have thought of a solution around this. To start with, we will not use cash transactions on our platform. We will use bitcoin to pay the loyalty points, we will use an ICO – initial coin offering to raise the money for this project," Satvik said.

"What is ICO?" Ashok asked.

"Oh, so you guys have not been following up the recent advancement in technology – Blockchain, a distributed ledger concept where all transactions are recorded in a transparent way without the need of a central agency. It is, in a way, an alternate banking system without the need of any central bank. This concept is revolutionary when it comes to sharing data access across many people, a perfect platform for something like Paybook. The post likes and engagements can be rewarded in the form of bitcoins.

"ICO – initial coin offering is a funding program where investors provide initial capital for the project and are offered bitcoins in return. These bitcoins eventually appreciate with time, benefiting the investors. It is the new avatar of IPO in the digital currency world. A lot of startups in the western countries are using this route to generate capital and create value," Satvik seemed to have researched on this topic.

"After one year, these bitcoins can be converted to actual cash. So, till one-year bitcoin will act as our surrogate money," he added further.

"But hang on, isn't it a kind of indirect betting in the form of social media, some kind of Ponzi scheme that we hear every other day?" Sandeep questioned the intent.

"You can call it whatever, but currently there is no such label for such an idea, and it is not illegal. If we do not do it, someone else will do it. If you guys are willing to join me in this, we can make it a great success. It may sound crazy in the beginning, but so must have been Facebook when it started. Even the people's behaviors change with time, who would have thought that people would happily share their personal photographs with unknown people," Satvik was convinced about the eventual success of Paybook.

"But people are already hooked on Facebook and it is pretty much fulfilling their social needs why would they shift to a new platform like Paybook?" Ashok asked.

"Because, currently Facebook browsing is really a wasteful activity, many people spend hours every day writing new posts, creating content and browsing but do they earn anything out of it? Even though it may look free, it is not free. We are all working for Facebook to enrich their platform to be used by the advertisers. Today there is still some novelty with social media, so people visit it for fun and curiosity. But soon they will lose interest in Facebook.

"Think of a market where you go every day to present your product (your content in this case) but don't get any money out of it. Instead, the advertisers sell you the products while you are browsing social media. Will you ever go to such a market for a long time? You will go there for the first few days just for curiosity but will discontinue that soon. On Facebook today, people are spending their time, sharing their data and creating value out of it but they don't get any remuneration," Satvik tried to convince his other two friends.

"If it is such a wasteful activity, I am sure sooner or later, people will realize that and stop using social media. Our whole business proposition of Paybook is based on the premise that people will continue to use social media. People are getting increasingly busy these days?" Ashok was still skeptical of the proposition.

"People getting increasingly busy is the biggest fallacy of our time because technology today is automating everything. If you observe carefully, we have a lot freer time today that we don't know what to do with. We can shop on the click of a button, travel to places in a matter of a few hours and almost get all the work done by various service providers.

"With the rise of automation and artificial intelligence, even our work lives will shrink further. We may not have to work so hard to achieve the same outcome. That is why people are spending more time on social media today. In fact, I believe society will have a unique problem to engage increasingly free people," Satvik gave a long justification.

"There are only two ways you can engage this unemployable useless class -either give them drugs or keep them busy in virtual reality. Our app actually fits well for the second option," replied Sandeep.

"But what impact will it have on people – wouldn't it harm them in some way?" asked Ashok.

"In business, you can't always take a moralistic view. If it is not illegal, we should be fine. One last time – are you guys in it or not?" Satvik felt exasperated after explaining the same thing several times.

"We are in," both Sandeep and Ashok said in unison.

Even though Ashok and Sandeep were not fully convinced about the efficacy of the idea, they had faith in Satvik's determination. He had not changed his intrinsic character since the college days. Once he set his eyes on a goal, he was never shy of putting the extra effort. He was always the leader, this time, he had the vision to give shape to his ideas.

Sandeep thought this could be a good platform to test his technology skills. Suddenly the face of Mark Zuckerberg flashed in front of his eyes, was this his moment? All big ideas start small, maybe Paybook was the one for them.

He spoke to his PhD guide, Roman.

"This is a fantastic idea. My own research says that an application like that will be a big hit among people. I am excited about it for another reason though – data. Data is the new oil in the digital age. Anything that helps you capture people's data will be of great value. I will help you create an intelligent algorithm that can predict the user behavior," Roman encouraged Sandeep to go for the same.

Ashok, on the other hand, thought to shed his skepticism of the new age social media for once. His party had recently started a renewed drive to use technology to create a more extensive support base. Maybe this was the time to take the plunge for Ashok.

"If this venture works out well, one day I will also introduce this to my party people who can earn some easy money," he thought.

Second Life

"How was your vacation Satvik, meeting your college buddies after so many years?" Shalini asked when he returned home after 4 days of Goa trip.

"It was loads of fun, as anticipated. It was nice to go back in time and talk about those good old days," replied Satvik.

"Especially when your family is not around, isn't it? I guess you all must have partied as if there was no tomorrow. Didn't you all drink all night and go for pub hopping?"

"No, no, we only had orange juice and mostly visited the temples"- giggled Satvik then added- "of course, we enjoyed our time, but this trip was memorable for another reason. In fact, we chanced upon a startup idea and all three of us signed up to work towards it. It was a great outcome in the end," replied Satvik.

"Then good that I did not come along, how boring it must have been discussing a business idea in a party-like setup of Goa beaches."

"This idea will interest everyone, including you. It is something that we all spend most of our free time on – social media," said Satvik.

"Don't tell me you guys have dreamt about another Facebook, a copycat idea," joked Shalini.

"We have planned to set up a new social networking site that will pay people to have fun. Think again, people can earn money from social media. So, we will indirectly employ many people, including you and all your Facebook friends," Satvik replied.

"That sounds like weird but appealing if true, all of my friends would be really happy to hear about a social media site like this. That looks like a one-stop solution for the unemployment problem for the entire country," replied Shalini.

"I know it sounds ludicrous but let me explain. Three of us are planning to set up a new social media company called Paybook – the name says it all," said Satvik.

"Even Ambani will go broke if he pays everyone for doing nothing and wasting time on social media. Who is going to finance the same? Are your friends going to be a partner in the company?" asked Shalini while taking away the remote of the TV from his hand.

This looked like one of those crazy ideas that Satvik used to have on Friday evening after coming from office - tired and exhausted. Most of those ideas vanished by Monday when he had to go to the office again.

"Since it was my idea and I have thought most of the details, I will be the head of the company. But don't worry, I have worked a clever business plan for the same. It will be self-funded," replied Satvik.

"We needed some tech wizard who could help create a great technology platform. Sandeep has done a PhD from Germany in the IT field. He has always been a tech geek. He can spend days programming. He will be our technology man of the company," Satvik said further.

"But what about Ashok, he is not even in the field of technology?"

"Because he has good political connections. You may not know, but his uncle is a prominent leader of the communist party. Ashok himself has been very active in politics though he has not won any election. He can help us reach out to the right people and get things done."

"But you only told me that he was the only one in your batch who could not complete his degree and was thrown out of the college after six years."

"As I said, we are not making him the business partner for his business or technology skills. We need him to get the things done for us, to get the license and even to mobilize opinion in our favor in the government and media," replied Satvik.

"But what's in it for him? What will he gain from working with you folks in a nondescript startup?" asked Shalini.

"Though our company will not be big, it will employ quite a few people – some as the test users and some as employees. Ashok is not winning elections; he must do something to establish himself as the leader. He has promised jobs to some of his party folks, he will be our operations manager responsible for all the logistics and running of the company. It is a win-win for all of us," replied Satvik.

"And once again I am asking, who is funding the company?"

"I and Sandy to start with, in fact, Sandy is putting 60% of the initial fund. Ashok has said that he will get the investors but only when our company is in action. He knows many businessmen and media people to create the right impact. More than money we need the word of mouth advertisement for common users."

"Have you gone mad?"- Shalini yelled at Satvik - "We don't even have enough money to buy our own house. Our household expense will only grow in future and you are risking the limited savings on some crazy idea!"

Satvik knew that this would be the first reaction of his wife, that is why he was reluctant to share the cost details. While she wished for the financial stability, a move like this would just throw the things off gear.

"The right time to start a venture is not when you have enough money but when you have the right idea and the passion for following your dream," Satvik replied.

"Such motivational quotes only look good in the books, not in practice. You are taking a big risk financially. Secondly, you forget that after your college days you did not keep in touch with Ashok and Sandeep. I will caution you that people change after college days."

"Any new business needs trust among the partners, I think we have something to start with and build on," Satvik looked determined.

"I had another idea. Why not you also join us in setting up the company, something like an HR manager? You can also test our app and give recommendations based on the user experience. I will have more support and confidence in the success," asked Satvik.

Satvik had learned this over time. The best way to handle the criticism is to make the criticizer a partner in the act. He knew Shalini's obsession with social media. This offer was too tempting for her.

"It seems you have planned it well, anyway I will be one of your first users of the platform. But you would have to take permission from your partners for this, wouldn't you?" Shalini's mood changed from skepticism to collaboration.

"I think you missed the part that I am the head of the new company. I can surely recommend an HR person, more so when she happens to be my wife."

Shalini also was now on board with the plan.

It is one thing to have an idea and another thing to take it to execution. The three friends, however, were super excited to make it happen. Ashok and Sandeep moved to Mumbai. They started passionately discussing for hours the pros and cons of every decision.

"I have looked around the last few days to find the best place for our office, and I came to the conclusion that it could be our party office in Andheri," said Ashok.

"I think we should look for an alternate place, which is more office like, maybe somewhere in BKC," said Satvik.

"Finally, yes, but that will take time. We can start in this office in the meanwhile. Don't worry, it is not used by any of our party workers currently," assured Ashok.

"If your party keep losing elections, the office space will always be available for alternate use," Satvik pulled Ashok's leg.

Satvik and Sandeep were quite surprised at the enthusiasm that Ashok was showing in this venture after initial resistance.

"Our users will never know where the office is, they would never need to know also. This is one good thing with these new ages mobile apps," added Sandeep.

"Ok, at least this will not cost us money, correct?" asked Satvik.

"Two of you are investing money directly, it is my way of sharing the financial burden," replied Ashok.

"One more thing"- said Satvik -"My wife Shalini was also excited about this idea and has agreed to work as the HR manager. She worked in a similar role earlier in another IT company. Moreover, she can also be an avid tester and provide feedback on our product usage."

"But hiring key personnel was agreed to be my job, wasn't it Satvik?" asked Ashok.

"Of course, it was, that is why I have put this proposal. I am sure you will approve of it. It is just one position of HR manager," replied Satvik.

"A CEO's wife will be no less powerful than the CEO whichever role we try to fit her in," Sandeep smiled when he said that.

"We have just divided the roles for the sake of convenience. Otherwise, we are all equal, just like friends," replied Satvik.

"Ok, she can work with us but do keep in mind that I am working on getting the right people for the job. A lot of qualified people have approached me. This was one of the conditions that we got the party office for temporary use," replied Ashok.

The burden of giving the idea the shape, squarely fell on Sandeep, thanks to his reputation as a tech wizard. It was easy to arrange for the office space and some finances but creating the next generation of social media proved to be too daunting a task for Sandeep.

"Satvik – though we have discussed the business idea, I am still not clear about the product that we are planning to build. I am also not clear how to go about it. Another Facebook type product will just be a dumb copycat idea," suggested Sandeep.

"Sandy, you are our technical wizard, you have to make it happen. Let me explain once again," replied Satvik.

"You remember our visit to casinos in Goa?"

"How can I forget that? After all, I lost five thousand rupees in the slot machine and I could have lost more had you guys not stopped me," replied Sandeep.

"Exactly, I want to create a slot machine type product in the social networking site. See even though people throng casinos hoping to hit the jackpots and occasionally they win as well, casinos don't lose money. We need to create an app where the odds of earning money is stacked against the users, but they are not aware. The key thing is that it should be tempting," replied Satvik.

"I thought about it Satvik, I somehow think it will not work. There is nothing remarkable about this idea," replied Sandeep.

"Don't tell me at this stage that our idea is bogus."

"I was thinking of something more substantive. See today most of us are not happy because we can't control most of the things. People and events around us are not exactly according to our liking. This creates stress in all of us, and we want to escape from the real world," replied Sandeep.

"Yes, we all want to live in a world where everything happens exactly as we want, it does not matter whether that is real or virtual," replied Satvik.

"Absolutely, if you want to make Paybook really immersive there is even a better option than gambling – it is called virtual reality. My research in PhD was exactly in this area," Sandeep replied.

"How exactly will that work?"

"Have you heard of something called Second Life, it preceded the era of Facebook and was slated to take the gaming industry by storm, just that it was not a game. It was real life like setup without any specific goal, unlike a game."

"How does that work and why people would prefer that?" asked Satvik.

"Second life was 'digital life in a way'. When it was launched, some people predicted this was the invention of the century."

"If you look at social media as something to create and share experience, virtual reality fits this perfectly. You can choose an avatar, interact with other people real or virtual, conduct your business and even earn money. For example, you can create a virtual house in second life and sell it to another fellow inhabitant or rent it out. Just like in real life, you can have friends and acquaintances, you can fall in love and have children," explained Sandeep.

"But it is still not clear to me why people would want to experience that instead of the real physical world?" asked Satvik.

"Coming back to our point of control, it can help you to escape the real world into your self-created dreamland where things will happen as per your wishes. It can create a sense of control that we all are running after. In real life, your wife may not listen to you but in Second life it does not happen like that," replied Sandeep.

"Think of an old lady who does not look as beautiful as when she was young. In second life she can still be her younger self. Everyone can live an aspirational life which in real life can never be possible," explained Sandeep

"I can understand your point. We all experience our lives in our mind. If we can recreate that experience through virtual reality, it can be more powerful than the real-world experience," concurred Satvik.

"If 'second life' was such a sensation why it never became as popular as Facebook," asked Satvik.

"I think it was ahead of its time and technology was not adequate."

Sandeep knew that social VR was the next revolution in this area. If this offering could be incentivized well for the users and supported by a sustainable business model, it could give Facebook a run for money. There was one more success criterion for this idea – identification for a small portable device that can transport people into the virtual world from the comfort of their homes, not the bulky gaming device at video game parlor that made people look like a zombie. Just like mobiles brought the revolution in the digital world, a handy device could make the VR easy to adopt. He was aware that there were few Chinese companies working in this area.

The Paybook idea that started like a second-generation Facebook was looking, even more, promising with the possibility of adding virtual reality.

"So, we read that an average person spends thirty minutes of his time daily on Facebook, right?" asked Satvik.

"With our virtual reality-based Paybook, most of the users will be so engaged that they would hardly have even thirty minutes available to do their worldly tasks. For the rest of the time, they will be immersed in our game."

"That looks scary as well. The human civilization will come to an end if anything like that happens ever. People choosing to be in the virtual world over the real world," said Satvik.

"Religion is the best example of virtual reality and you can see how much intoxicating it is for many people. It provides them meaning and purpose in life. The human mind does not differentiate between virtual and real. It just needs a good story to believe in. All we need to do is to gamify our new app so that the mind never remains idle – just like different levels in the game. It is all about brain science," replied Sandeep.

Launching Paybook

The first prototype of Paybook was like Facebook with a virtual bank. The social media interactions were equivalent to banking transactions, and virtual net worth was visible online along with other contacts. This looked ordinary, but it was a powerful mind concept that could attract all age groups.

"This will also be a place where the real and virtual world get fused into one – a sort of digital life for us," said Satvik.

"Absolutely, people can either choose their real self or can choose a digital avatar of their own liking."

"This is how the virtual life can be linked with real money, and this can be damn addictive I can tell you," Sandeep said.

But the most critical question was still staring at them – how to reach out to the potential users at the mass scale?

"Shall we advertise in newspapers and on television?" Ashok asked inquisitively.

"Have you ever seen Facebook or Google advertising in a newspaper or TV? Did we ever know when WhatsApp was launched before we all started using? These apps spread by word of mouth from users, just like a new addictive drug in the market. They are not like the new soap or perfume that can be launched in the traditional media," Satvik responded.

"We don't even have money to spend on these things. We will have to think of an innovate approach," Sandeep said.

"I have an idea" - said Shalini - "Why don't we launch Paybook first among our residents' association group. They can be the perfect guinea pig for our idea. Dubey uncle, who is our president is super enthusiastic in adopting anything new."

"We want to build a product for the new generation, no point in testing it with aged RWA members," Satvik said.

"But if we talk about money and investments with a little bit of fun, they might be interested. If we convince them that their money can grow 2-3 times in two years when their lock-in period will end, they will go for it definitely," Shalini tried to explain.

In the next association meeting, Paybook was launched with a lot of fanfare. Dubey uncle presented a symbolic check of Rs 10,000 bitcoin equivalents to every member.

"This is just the initial gift, mind you. Based on your social media engagements, it can grow in multiples. At the end of two years, you can choose to cash out your entire worth," he proudly announced.

Shalini was very keen to show this to her friends. If nothing else this earned her some bragging rights in the kitty party group for introducing a cool thing.

"For the first time you have a social networking site that will pay you to have fun, now no one can tell us that we waste our time on social media," Shalini showed this proudly to her friends.

"All that you have to do is remain logged into the site, and post content that will be liked by others, you can even earn money by engaging with other's posts. There will be product reviews and surveys from the companies as well that can help us earn money. You can introduce your friends and acquaintances that can help you earn more," she explained further.

"We have seen many such ideas in the past, most of them turn out to be not so successful. There is a company called 'Amway' that is entirely created using this model. The only difference, in this case, is that you are using social media," replied one of her friends.

"See for any entertainment today, you have to pay money. Paybook will be the only platform that will pay you while also providing an element of fun just like Facebook," elaborated Shalini.

"The payment part is too good to believe. How will the payment be made?" asked Sheela, who used to work in a bank earlier.

"The payment will be made in bitcoin, a virtual currency that is making news these days. These currencies can be traded among the members," Shalini explained what Sandeep had told her during the product development.

"In that case, it will be of little use because it can't be accepted in the real world," retorted Sheela.

"Paybook also has an option to convert the bitcoin into real currency at a discount after two years. However, you would all understand slowly that it is wise to keep the money in the bitcoin as it may appreciate much faster than the real currency."

Sheela was still not convinced, it did not stop other friends from believing that it was a really a good idea to give it a try, after all, it did not cost any money and had the possibility of earning something, however remote.

Dubey uncle finally said, "The resident group badly need something that could help increase the interactions among members. The resident welfare activities are thought to be the most boring thing ever, no one even checks the mail or message sent in the group. People hardly turn up even for the yearly election, leave aside discussing the prime issues concerning us. Few of us who invest our personal time to fix the community problems do not even get appreciation for the same – people consider it a thankless job. The idea that the members can get paid for society level engagement on Paybook might bring people on board."

Just as Paybook needed some willing participants, the association members looked for something cool like this. It took off very well.

"We can run the makeshift office of Paybook without funding for some days, but soon we will require external investment to survive. Do you think anyone will really invest in an idea like this which has little chance of being profitable?" Sandeep asked.

"Do you know which company is growing fastest today?"

"Possibly Amazon," replied Sandeep.

"Yes, the investors love it. Even though the company is not profitable and hardly pays a dividend, the investors don't mind pumping more and more money into it. You know why?"

"Because Amazon tells a story that everyone loves to hear. If the story is exciting, investors do not mind even supporting a loss-making business. Amazon has mastered this art over time. People do not invest in the present, they invest in future dreams. We need to create a compelling dream for people to believe in," explained Satvik in detail.

According to Satvik, the business model of Paybook was compelling.

The tagline of Paybook was – **earn while you have fun**. The initial response was lukewarm, but soon people were attracted to the idea with the promise of making some money. Within six months, Paybook acquired a customer base of more than five lakhs.

The transaction behavior of the members was interesting – to start with, not many would show any activity on the platform. They would just passively browse through, waiting for others to make the first move. But with time, it started picking. The thought that each like was money, in a way, made the whole social media experience even more interesting. It was not only fun and entertainment but some business as well. Even people who were otherwise a mute spectator on Facebook started engaging on Paybook.

Some of the engagements were mutual admiration – "I like your post hoping you would like mine." It served both the purpose – vanity and money. Though the money earned was virtual, it took away the impression of social media browsing being a complete waste of time.

Paybook got very extensive coverage in the media articles. It was touted as one of the most successful startups in India ever. It was timed well as many social media users, and even regulators wanted an Indian version of Facebook.

But Satvik was not satisfied with the little progress that Paybook was making. He wanted to move into the next orbit.

"Users can sell one of the biggest assets that all of them have, and it is not yet monetized because we are not aware of the value of the same. The data is the new age oil, the users can sell their personal data to us, and we can, in turn, sell to various companies for a premium. The product and marketing companies need access to user data and behavior to gain insight. Many times, we don't realize that the trail of digital information that we generate has real value and can be sold at a price."

"But would that not be a violation of privacy?" Sandy asked.

"See data ownership is a fuzzy area. Who owns the data generated by a user if not him or her? Moreover, data privacy is an issue if a company sells the data of users without passing on any benefit to the users. If a user shares the data willingly for a price, it becomes a legitimate sale like anything else. Do you see my point?" Satvik explained the idea further.

"Well what you are saying is, we will tell the users that we will pay them for sharing their personal data and sell them to willing companies – complete transparency in that way – no pretense," Sandeep was able to understand the master plan slowly.

Taste of Success

The idea that germinated in Goa one year back as part of a friendly meet was turning out to be a great success. The user enrollment at Paybook was hitting a record every day. Word of mouth had spread from the limited experiment at the housing society to include different user groups.

The three friends worked very hard for the last year to achieve all this. They had become sort of celebrity trio who set the social media on fire in India. There was no better way to celebrate the occasion than to raise a toast at the same place in Goa. It was somehow turning out to be a lucky ideation place for them.

"Sir, where do you want to go?" 2-3 taxi drivers approached the friends as soon as they arrived at the airport.

"Near Bagha beach."

"It will cost 1500 rupees sir; it is quite far from here."

After some initial haggling, they settled for 1300 rupees.

"My wife was telling me that all of her friends have moved to Paybook and they love it," Satvik said.

"Yes Satvik, even I heard similar things from many of my friends and families," Sandeep replied.

"You guys know Dubey uncle, the septuagenarian president of our association? He was saying that Paybook has been an amazing thing for him and his wife," replied Satvik.

"And we thought that the elders would be the last to adopt our product."

"He stays with his wife; his kids have all grown up, and they live in different cities — a typical empty nest syndrome that we see these days. Their favorite pastime earlier was to talk about their younger days. This always made them pensive and despondent.

"With Paybook, they are experiencing their adulthood once again rather than just talking about them. Dubey uncle and his wife both have digital avatars as their second lives. They interact with other digital avatars, enjoy social activities there and even have parties. Unlike real life, they say there is no discrimination in the virtual world due to age. Today they can't go to a pub, but they can go to a virtual pub. It has been a great experience, they say.

"Digital life is more exciting for the elders if they really get hooked on to it. These days even the young kids do not listen to their parents, but in Paybook, they can create the world of their own and control things as they want. The best thing is they do not need to do any physical activity to keep their minds engaged," said Satvik.

"Even as our body becomes weak with old age, our mind does not stop growing. So, the brain needs engagement until we are alive. Our virtual reality game is a fantastic avenue for the same. It helps them find some purpose and meaning in their day to day life. This makes them happy eventually, and they can live even longer," Sandeep replied.

"Actually, people who were not in active jobs were the first to move to our platform, and even today they are the most active ones. They include people like housewives and some of the young adults who are yet to be employed. Now they believe that they are earning some money," Ashok also added.

"Sometimes, I feel that we have opened a virtual casino and employed people there to gamble in their free time," Sandy said.

"Yes, remember the marbles game that I was talking about earlier? As kids, the marble game was so addictive. When I lost the marbles in the game, I borrowed from other friends and kept playing, hoping to win. When I won, I thought it was my day, and I should capitalize on the same. In any case, I was playing endlessly unless my mother shouted at me to stop. Sometimes my mother would throw the marbles away, I had to hide them in a safe corner," Ashok remembered.

"Yes, but here no one needs to hide the marbles that they win from our Paybook. They are virtual points – safe, secure and far more fun than the marbles," replied Satvik.

"Let us raise the toast," Satvik gently touched his beer-filled glass with the one held by Sandeep

"You know guys – we create technology that changes us, the way we think, talk, and behave. Do we recall how the way we communicate has changed in our lifetimes – especially the remote communication?"

"Yes, as a child, I recall that the only way to communicate with our grandparents who stayed in the village was through the letters. Those envelopes and postcards used to be the fastest way to send information to far off places. But I must tell you, those letters had some life in them. I still have some of the old letters that my father wrote to me when we were in college. Those handwritten letters had an emotional connection that we miss today, the practice of writing letters has disappeared," Ashok agreed.

"Although it used to take many days for the snail mail to reach, we were pretty content with it. It never seemed like a pressing problem – even urgent information could wait for days and we had adjusted ourselves to that."

"Exactly – then the telephone came. That black colored heavy instrument was the greatest asset any household could have. The entire neighborhood depended on it," Satvik said.

"Yes, and it was quite funny at times, we were the first in our neighborhood to have the phone in our house. Our phone number was circulated to everyone in the surroundings who would eventually share this with their relatives. It became an act of social service for us to receive the calls of relatives of neighbors. Receiving the call was free, so it there was no way we could have been discourteous to our neighbors by refusing them," replied Sandeep.

"And there was a lucrative business model built around it – remember the STD booth, today people will have to google to find out how exactly it looked like.

"Many of our friends looked at this as an alternative source of livelihood. The yellow-colored STD booths were the most common sights in the big and small cities in the 1990s," said Satvik.

"And you could never miss the long queue outside those booths."

"The weird thing was that people waited outside these booths for hours for the right time as the charge rates were different at different times in the day. The late-night calls were cheaper, so it made more sense for people to call at late night even if it meant some inconvenience to the receiver of the call."

"All this was a part of our lives just a couple of decades back, but today it looks like they never existed. In today's world of mobile, Facebook and WhatsApp, we wonder how we managed then. Today if we don't hear back from our kids for a few minutes we get anxious – but our grandparents never heard from our parents for days and months, and still, they were not anxious. We invent technologies that invent a different human in us," Ashok said.

"That is why I say that technology has changed our mind. The way we feel happy, sad, and anxious is, to a large extent, the outcome of the technology that we use. But we need not be worried about it, we need to welcome these changes – our brainchild Paybook is an opportunity of such technological evolutions," Satvik felt proud that they were riding the wave at the right time.

"Elon Musk says that soon we may need an artificial digital plug-in on top of our brain cortex that can directly connect to the internet using high-speed wireless. Our thoughts will depend on the speed of internet downloads," replied Sandeep.

"No need to learn anything for humans in that case, kids will not have to go to school either," laughed Ashok.

"We will not require to communicate; we will just exchange thoughts like telepathy. We can download our brain to a powerful computer for processing overnight while we sleep peacefully. In the morning, we can re-upload the processed data of the computer to our brain," said Sandeep.

"So soon we all will become cyborgs – when the internet merges with us. We will all be connected like the internet of brains. It will be hard to imagine what it means to be human in that era. Thankfully we are not yet there. Personally, I would refuse to exist in that situation," said Ashok.

"Experts say increasingly many of the cognitive jobs can be done more efficiently by Artificial Intelligence. This will effectively result in humans losing even their current cognitive abilities. These humans will automatically get downgraded to housecat that can only play video games all day," said Sandeep.

"So, while the machines are learning today, humans are getting hooked to their cell phones and becoming dumber. As true futurists, we have already developed something for our people at that time. Paybook will be handy for keeping people busy while still being a dumb house cat," Satvik never left an opportunity to pat himself.

The drive from the new airport was very refreshing. For a long distance, the roads followed the natural coastlines covered by rich vegetation. There were quite a few ship-building spots along the way. The ships had unique names. Some of them looked very old, left unattended in that dilapidated condition.

"Look at that ship – it reads 'Social media rehab center'," Ashok pointed at one large ship anchored at the shore.

"That name is quite intriguing, I want to go there. I have never seen anything like that. Does it also include our Paybook – we must check out," Satvik asked the taxi driver to go near it and stop for a while.

"Sir, some of these ships are rented out for private business, sometimes of dubious nature. It may not be safe for you guys to trespass," the taxi driver said.

But Satvik was insistent. Even Sandeep was curious to know. After agreeing for some additional fare for the stoppage time, the taxi driver stopped near the entrance of the ship.

A signboard read –

> *"If social media has hacked your life and you are trying to reclaim it, you are in the right place. We use state of the art approach to detox your brain from technology superbugs."*

Their curiosity increased further, and they decided to walk into the ship. Inside the ship, there was a vast open sitting area, but no one was there. Satvik noticed a person, sitting in the other corner alone – perhaps in a state of meditation and unaware of the three friends approaching him.

"He must be the instructor and the person behind this unique concept," Satvik was very curious to speak to him.

"He might get angry if we disturb him."

"We will wait till he finishes; he might provide us with the most important insights for the business we are in. I have a weird feeling that I have met him earlier," said Satvik.

After waiting for the fifteen minutes, the person opened his eyes and greeted the three visitors calmly.

"We saw this interesting signboard, so we were curious. Aren't you afraid of being here alone on this large ship?" Satvik asked.

"Why should I be afraid, I don't have anything that a thief or robber would be interested in. I enjoy sitting here, I am alone but not lonely. In fact, sitting in this disconnected, lonely setup, I believe that I have rejuvenated my life," replied the person.

"But this place is frequented by many people when we run our courses. They love this place and what they learn here," he added.

"What is this course about?"

"This course is a cure for digital life that has enslaved all of us. We practice mindfulness and meditation in this secluded place. You may feel it is boring, but this is how you connect with your real self. People find peace here, away from the cacophony that you would have experienced on the crowded beach," the person replied.

70

"What kind of people attend such courses?"

"We do a small test for the participants before enrolling into this course. Those who come here, we ask them to throw their cell phones from this ship deck into the bushes below."

"It so deep and dense, I think it would get lost," replied Ashok looking down from the deck.

"We tell them our boys usually find them, but they take 4-5 days. There is also a remote possibility that it may get lost. Those who fail this test gets enrolled here," replied the person.

"Hang on – something like this also happened to us in Bagha beach where a person who looked like a drug addict gave us the same challenge – to throw the phone into the sea. Are you the same person?" Satvik asked.

"I don't recall anything – but you may be right. A year back, I was very much like a lost person, I had no interest in life. I was living in a trance. I don't recall anyone whom I might have met during that period," the man in his late 30s replied calmly.

"Last time we met, you challenged us to throw our mobile phones, we were scared and walked past thinking of you a mad person. Today you seem to be a guru," Satvik said.

"Yes, I have recovered from madness, a little bit of that is gripping everyone today. We are losing ourselves slowly."

"We three are school friends who have come here to celebrate the success of our company – Paybook. It is the virtual reality revolution of social media; it also pays the user for being active in the social media," Satvik mentioned proudly.

"I am not on social media anymore, but I have heard about Paybook from many people. I think it is getting even more popular than Facebook. You have taken the addiction to another level by making it more like social gambling."

71

"You seem to have very negative views about social media?"

"We usually have social media addicts as visitors. They are like drug addicts. Today it looks like I am meeting the drug peddlers who create such things that harm people," replied the man.

"You are being so harsh to Paybook and the genuine success it has brought to us," replied Satvik.

"Even the drug seller says that they help people in forgetting their pain. It gives happiness to them. The only problem is that it is at the cost of something even more basic – our lives."

Perils of Addiction

"Our short conversation has made me even more curious to know - how did this idea occur to you – 'social media rehab'?" asked Satvik.

"This is a long story of my personal life; you may find it relevant in the context of Paybook."

"My name is Ramesh. I am a neurosurgeon. I have studied the function of our brain, perhaps the most complex thing on this earth. I had a private clinic in Andheri, Mumbai. I was doing phenomenally well by all standard, my clinic was very well known in the surroundings."

"From being a doctor to social media counselor is a stark transition," said Ashok.

"Yes, I set up the clinic over a period and hired few doctors, it was my dream come true. In just 3-4 years it expanded so well that we were planning to open a full-fledged hospital," Ramesh explained further.

"Thanks to my busy schedule, I was not able to devote much time for my own family, particularly my son, who was growing into teens. Like all doting father, I used to feel guilty for not spending enough time with my son. I used to overcome that guilt by providing for whatever my young son asked for – toys or gadgets. I soon realized that I had bought him several video games that he liked to play. As he grew, he started getting more and more involved in those games," said Ramesh.

"Yes, these days the kids are quite addicted to these screen games. Our times, our parents used to shout at us to stay indoors. Now it is the other way around – we have to force the kids to go out to play in the playground," Satvik said.

"But this is not a new problem today. Remember when the TV sets came into our households in the 90s, we were all glued to it. Even earlier during the 1980s, BBC in Britain ran a program called 'Why Don't You' that cajoled the kids to step out of their house and play in the open field. The tagline of the program was 'turn off your TV sets and do something less boring instead'."

"This problem has indeed been there earlier also, just that now it is going to the clinical levels," replied Ramesh.

"I still remember my son was overjoyed when my wife gifted him a Samsung smartphone on his 15th birthday. It was something he had been asking for many months but fearing his addiction I was somehow postponing that. My son kept insisting that he needed the phone, not for fun but for study purposes as well.

"These days, students also share study conversation on WhatsApp. If you want me to do better, a smartphone is needed', my son used to plead."

"While I was skeptical of social media, my wife did not think it was such a bad idea. She herself used to spend hours on Facebook and WhatsApp. I never bothered too much about her obsession with social media but very well knew that this could be far more detrimental for the teens.

"Are you keeping a tab on his usage of the phone?" I used to ask my wife.

"How can I keep tab all the time, these days the kids don't appreciate their parents watching over their shoulder for such things," she would typically reply.

I was observing that my son was getting more addicted each day. His performance in the school also started deteriorating.

"What is the password for your screen lock," I asked him once.

"Papa, you are becoming too intrusive. No one shares phone password with their parents. You see, even mom does not share with you, does she? You will have to treat me as an adult," my son used to reply to the same.

"He was right - despite my repeated attempts, my wife would never share things like password of her phone. It was becoming somewhat secretive. While on one hand, social media brought the world together by connecting them, here it was creating a barrier for our own trust. The same Facebook that connects can disconnect close relations as well.

"I still can't forget the first day of the New Year. Though it was a holiday for many hospitals, our clinic was still operational. We had a busy day as usual. I was about to start surgery when my wife called me.

"There is an emergency at home — can you come immediately?" she told me, and her tone was very nervous and panicky. She was crying incessantly.

"It was 10 am in the morning. I was about to start surgery in an hour. But I told my colleague that I may not be able to attend the same. I feared there was something terribly wrong after the call. My colleagues had never seen me leaving an emergency operation like this."

"I immediately got into my car; I was getting worried. I tried calling my wife many times, but she did not receive my call. My heart sank – what could have happened?"

"When I reached near my apartment, there was a small crowd there. Most of the people were not familiar. I parked my car on the side and stepped out to find what the issue was.

"A boy has committed suicide by jumping off from the 6ᵗʰ floor of this apartment," one of the persons said.

"I lived on the sixth floor – I recalled my wife's crying voice. It was too difficult for me to bear the truth anymore. I fainted and did know what happened for the next few hours. I don't want to sadden you all by describing the gory detail of the event, but this was the moment when my entire world came crashing down," Ramesh said that with inconsolable grief.

"Heartbreaking, I am sorry to hear about this. But why did he take such a tragic step?" asked Ashok.

"We were equally surprised; we had never observed any such tendency in him. We were surprised to see various cut marks on this body. One of them was a picture of a fish made on his wrist," Ramesh explained.

"Oh my god, was he a victim of Blue Whale Game?" asked Satvik.

"Possibly yes, we would never know for sure, but he was into some social game that prompted him to do something like this. The Blue Whale, as the name signifies is a suicide game where the victim usually in the early teens, is given a task every day for 50 days. It starts with seemingly easy tasks like watching a horror movie at 4 am and slowly degenerates to difficult tasks like making a mark of a blue whale by razor on your body and send the picture to the admin of the game who then sends another task. The final task is to commit suicide usually by jumping off from height," Ramesh replied.

"But why don't they quit the game when they realize that it is going to kill them. A 15-year-old child is smart enough to know that these days?" Satvik asked.

"After the incident, I did a lot of research about this game. This game was invented in Russia, and the inventor is in jail currently. What the game does is, to attract vulnerable teens who have low self-worth and are depression prone. Before they begin the game, they take the entire contact details of the kid, e.g. parents, schools, friends etc. First, they instill false confidence by giving them a simple task and encourage them for completing the same. Later, when the child realizes that he has been trapped in a dangerous situation and wants to quit, the game admin threatens to reveal the secret to the kid's parents, schools and friends. They use a tactic of stick and carrot to control the behavior of the child. They also psychologically mold the child slowly into believing what the game admin says. It is kind of hypnotizing the child and blackmailing for mental control."

"But what does the game admin gain out it, I am sure no one pays him for a teen committing suicide in some far-off place?" asked Ashok.

"You can ask the same question about serial murderers?" said Satvik.

"Exactly, these things are still a subject matter of research in psychology. Today you can find so many people who try to hack the sensitive systems just for the fun of it. They may not gain anything tangible out of it, but people get a kick and mental pleasure in the sufferings of others. Sometimes these people are driven by an ideology but many times they are just bored, talented people. At times they are driven to an extreme that you see some demented people shooting the innocent school kids. Some of these things are attributed to mental illness where people can't differentiate between video game and real life. I am a neurosurgeon, but our understanding of psychological illness is so limited that we can hardly answer why these people act in such ways," explained Ramesh.

"I think the government should ban the access of internet and social media for impressionable kids. The social media today is filled up with all kind of good and bad people who have amplified reach to almost everyone online. This also includes kids and vulnerable teens who can be a ready target for all kind of nefarious activities," said Ashok.

"It was not only the agony of my child's death; it was also the feeling of guilt that somehow I was responsible for the same. I remember the day I was insisting on getting the password for his phone. Just that if I had persisted with the same, I would have known what was happening to him. It was my negligence in some way, I was an absent father."

"This incident must have been devastating for your wife," asked Satvik.

"My wife started behaving quite weird after the incident. She was getting more and more withdrawn after the fateful event. I thought she was upset with me. So I let her take time to settle in.

"But slowly I realized that she was spending even more time on her phone. I thought she was vulnerable; she was trying to find refuge in the virtual world as the real world was too scary for her. I was not sure whether her social media addiction was helping her in forgetting the tragedy or making her more depressed every passing day. You can't share a sad incident on Facebook, no one does. So, browsing through social media when you are sad can make you even worse – you end up thinking that the whole world is happy except you. It can create a split personality even for the normal person.

"I was getting more worried about her. I had tried but she was least forthcoming in sharing her WhatsApp conversations and social media activities. She became even more secluded and withdrawn, at some point, she even stopped talking to me.

"Once, while she was asleep, I used her thumb impression to login to her phone. I knew it was not the right thing, but I had grown too cautious after the unfortunate incident. When I read through her WhatsApp messages, I was in a far bigger shock. I chanced upon some very intimate conversations that she regularly used to have with one of her school friends. The content of the message indicated that it was a serious affair and they were planning to marry soon. The history of the chat clearly showed that it was going on for the last 2 years.

"I was heart-broken, I felt more grief than the sad news of my son. Shall I confront her on this? What is the point now? The trust was not broken that day, it happened two years ago and probably it was way too late for any rapprochement. It was the end of our marriage – it ended two years earlier, just that I got to know about it that day.

"Earlier I was worried about her, now a sudden rage filled me – I was foolishly caring for someone who was essentially cheating on me. While I toiled day in and day out at my clinic, my son and wife had a world of their own in which I was absent. Social media, in a way, devastated my life completely," said Ramesh.

"In wee hours of the night, I quietly stepped out of the house. I left a note on the table for my wife.

> *I happened to read your WhatsApp messages. I don't know where things went wrong, but I am sure that we are at the point of no return. I am leaving this home and this city. I don't know my destination; I just want to wonder. I wish you all the best for your plans.*

"I left my home that night, never to return back. For several days these beaches in Goa were my home. I would roam around for hours in the darkness because I wanted to get lost in the darkness. I started drinking heavily and taking drugs.

They helped me forget my past and thus alleviate the pain somehow. When I was working in Mumbai, I had everything but time for myself and my family. Now I had a lot of free time to reflect. To my surprise, I realized that richness does not come from a busy life, true luxury is having free time," replied Ramesh.

"That could be the time we met you last year – you were looking like an addict and half-mad. You almost charged at us when we refused to throw away our mobiles," said Ashok.

"I was no longer the busy neurosurgeon of Andheri clinic. I had pressed the reset button of my life. Few times in your life, you must restart all over. I slowly forgot my previous life except for one thing. I was mad with anyone who was carrying a smartphone, I thought they were the cause of my miseries. I could see the society was slowly consuming this poison without being aware. It was changing our mind in a very negative way.

"Then one day, I decided that the best message I could carry from my personal misfortune was to dedicate the rest of my life for people to reclaim their lives from the social media. I saved a lot of people with my expertise in surgery, now it was time to study how our mind works and how it can be educated against this new-age digital menace. I realized this could be more helpful to the society," Ramesh added further.

"I sympathize with you for the unfortunate incidents. It is really heartbreaking; however, I do not concur with your conclusion. Social media is also a communication medium where people share their ideas and thinking. In earlier times, there used to town squares where all people assembled and discussed issues that concerned the society in general. It was a necessary meeting point where ideas clashed and converged.

Today, technology has made it even easier, you don't have to physically go to the town square. You can discuss that with the comfort of your living room," Satvik replied.

"Social media and Facebook are the last places that encourage development of new ideas. It is only like shouting out loud, but no one listens to the other person. It does not allow any ideological convergence at any stage," replied Ramesh.

"Some of the Facebook pages have millions of followers, any post by them is responded by hundreds of people; certainly, they lead fusion of different ideologies," Satvik replied.

"I have studied this subject in detail. We can also match it with our own experience. Based on our own preferences, we become members of the community Facebook pages that match those ideas. For example, if one has a specific viewpoint, he or she will be a member of scores of like-minded communities or follow people with similar ideologies. So eventually, the person will always see the content that only perpetuates his or her belief and will always ignore the ones that negate that. This is what leads to radicalization in ideas. If you see these days everyone is on the extreme side of ideologies with little moderation. That is why you would also see that people rarely change their ideological positions based on Facebook contents. Facebook is essentially killing the space of healthy discussion in our lives," Ramesh replied based on several studies that he was doing in this area.

"Just because guns kill people, they are not an object of hatred. Guns can be used for good purpose and the bad purpose. Similarly, smartphone and social media today can be used both ways," Satvik said.

"Exactly, when you buy a car, you need to learn how to drive it, else you would meet with an accident, and the car is not to be blamed for the same," Sandeep added further.

"You are right, for as much as you dislike there will always be guns in the society. All that you can do is to make people aware of how and where to use them. So, now I train people on how to use social media in moderation. That is why I run this social media rehab center."

"What is so unique about this?" asked Satvik.

"All my life, I studied human brains and how our day-to-day actions and thoughts are governed by the same. However, there is one more thing that we don't study in science – the human mind. In fact, the medical communities deny the existence of mind at all. But I have concluded that mind has the existence beyond the physical brain. It is the mind that ultimately gives direction to our lives. Unfortunately, we never even try to understand our own mind. My objective here is to make people aware of their own self by doing meditation and tapping into the power of mind or consciousness."

"That is what some of the religion teach, isn't it? But it has no scientific basis," said Ashok.

"Study of self-consciousness has less to do with religion and more to do with spirituality. It is a quest to understand the larger purpose and meaning in our lives. It is self-discovery on an unknown path. It is exploratory, and only the adventurous people undertake it. Religion is the opposite of the same in many ways. It provides you with pre-defined answers to stop your self-discovery," replied Ramesh.

"But how can that help someone? Do you tell them to stop using phone completely?" asked Satvik.

"No, I don't say that. In fact, for any addiction, I don't tell people to stop at all," replied Ramesh.

"Once a chain smoker came to me asking for help in this regard. I knew that the person was aware of the dangerous effect of smoking, else he would have never come to me. So, I told him not to quit smoking but continue the same but with one condition – increase his consciousness to a level that he could observe all his senses and experience the same.

"He went through several sessions of mindfulness training for 3 weeks here that helped elevate his numb senses. Then one day he came back saying – the cigarette tasted like chemical and smelled awful, it was repulsive and nauseating.

"He was right, the cigarette actually tests like bad chemical for the first-time smoker, but soon the brain overpowers all other senses and makes them numb. With time mind gets relegated to the background and brain impulses start ruling over."

"What I did was re-ignited those mindful senses that were made numb over a period. The same concept can be extended for social media addiction as well," replied Ramesh.

"That is an interesting concept – getting people rid of the digital intoxication, just like alcohol rehab centers. Do people really come to your center?" Satvik said.

"When I started this six-months back, many people laughed at the idea. They said these days when everybody was living a Facebook life, who would ever come to a center like this. But I was convinced of the ill-effects that it has on people. It slowly dumbs down your brain. It makes you feel depressed. Unknowingly it takes control of your awareness and you start living an empty life. The objective of my center is for people to reclaim their life thoughts and awareness. You would not believe; I have all kind of people coming into my rehab center, from the high-flying CEO who is depressed to students and housewives who spend hours on their smartphones. They thank me profusely at the end of the program."

"I recently read a matrimonial ad where one of the conditions was that the bride should not be addicted to social media," Ashok said.

"It has really reached clinical level, and if we do not do something, then we will all become zombies one day. Had I taken the right action, my own family would have been saved from the tragedy," concurred Ramesh.

It was a strange coincidence. While the three friends had come to celebrate the phenomenal success of their social media venture created a year ago, there was a case study of the impact of their work on real-life people. Ramesh's story was sad and none of the friends wanted that to happen in anyone's life.

"Do you think what we are doing with our company Paybook is detrimental to society, your story has made us think if we are doing something unethical? I warned Satvik in the beginning, but he was so bullish about the idea," asked Ashok.

"You are selling alcohol or cigarette, whether that is ethical or unethical is for you to interpret. It is legal and you are well within your rights to do the same. If not you someone else will do that. My objective is to make people aware of the ill effects of social media addiction and help them come out of it," replied Ramesh.

"Do you want to work with us, Ramesh? It may sound ironical, but I believe these two business concepts are complementary to each other. We encourage people to come on Paybook and for the ones that are clinically addicted, we refer them to your center. In fact, we can also provide you with data about who could be your potential customer. We need not say this publicly," enquired Satvik.

Satvik had spotted business opportunity even at these contradictory concepts. His mind was extra productive when it came to thinking of ways to make money. After all, it was he who had come up with the concept of Paybook that was turning out to be such a grand success.

"That would be like an alcohol company running a rehab center," replied Ramesh.

"I do believe that our business opportunities are complimentary. If not today, we would be glad to collaborate with you at some points later. I am sure our paths will cross again just like we met you one year back at the Bagha beach," said Satvik.

After this interesting conversation, the three friends bid goodbye to Ramesh. The taxi guy was mad at the hour-long wait.

When the three friends reached the resort, it was time to take a walk on the beach. The sunset at the Goa beach was amazing, like always. The bright red sun seemed like slowly sinking in the sea inch by inch. The beach was full of life – many people were taking selfies with the setting sun.

Making it Big

Ashok was not married; his entire time and energy were devoted to his party. His friends used to joke that he was married to his party instead. There are very few people who have a strong ideology and they live by that; Ashok was probably one of them. However, a few times, Sandeep had seen Ashok with a girl in his office.

"I tell you that tall girl is Ashok's secret girlfriend. I asked him a few times, but he dismissed saying she was just a party co-worker," Sandeep said.

"I have seen her as well, but she does not socialize much. When I bounced into her once she just gave me a blank look and passed by," said Satvik.

"Then you don't know that she is a social media star, she has thousands of followings on our Paybook. She can be our brand ambassador. Her posts are liked by thousands. She can influence people, a great asset to our party," replied Ashok when he overheard Satvik talking about Beny.

"You told me she is a professor in the city engineering college," said Sandeep.

"Yes, she is many persons rolled into one. She also does remarkable philanthropic work with some of the poor villagers. She fights for their rights. She encourages her students to visit those villages and work with tribal people for their development. Some of her work, at times, questions the ineffective approach of our government and local police. But she is never afraid of raising the right questions," replied Ashok.

"It is really brave and admirable for a woman to devote her life for such cause. I see her quite often in our office. What brings her here?" Satvik asked.

"She is of great help to our business. Due to her charity work, she gets a lot of funding within India and abroad. If we can convince her that our work benefits the poor section of society, she can even arrange funds for us," replied Ashok.

An upcoming startup needs only two things – customers and funding. Beny seemed to have leverage in both these areas. There was no way Satvik could have said no to a proposition like this.

"I don't doubt her intent, but going by her posts, she seems to have a very radical anti-government ideology. I am afraid that our platform will appear favoring one party," said Sandeep.

"Our party motto is to question the government when they fail in their duties. It should be everyone's duty for that reason. Beny is our leader who is working for the good of common people. If our Paybook can aid her objective of charitable work, it will be win-win for all."

"Paybook is not your party propaganda tool Ashok," Satvik got somewhat alarmed by this persistence.

"Let us not forget that the entire company is run by the staff provided by my party, and many of them have not even been paid. We have still not been able to move to another office that we had planned. If Paybook exists today, it is due to the generosity of my party," replied Ashok bluntly.

Though Ashok was a lesser partner in the beginning, he had acquired more importance in a very short time. Paybook was virtually running as per his direction and guidance. There was no way that Satvik could have countered Ashok on the day-to-day operation of the company.

As the head of HR, Shalini had seen a consistent rise in the volume of work in the last year. In the beginning, her work was only validating and testing the new features in Paybook and getting the feedback from her friends. Slowly she also started playing a more active role in other activities.

Paybook had expanded to a team of 25 people now. They all worked in the party office building with three floors; it was more like a residential apartment. Though there were no formal party activities, still Shalini saw some unknown visitors at times, so one room was blocked for them. Shalini thought this was also the time to expand the team further.

"Ashok, look at this resume. I want to hire this person for our increasing work in the HR department. I know her from my school days and she would be a good fit for our work," Shalini walked up to Ashok's desk who was still busy in some files.

"For all hiring, you just need to tell me, I can source the right profiles."

"But I can assure you this person could be most suited for this role, Ashok."

"That is not the point Shalini, it was agreed with Satvik and Sandeep at the time of setting up of Paybook that all hiring in this company will be done by me. That is the reason all employee functions report to me."

"And why was that?"

"See Shalini, I have got this space from my party on the pretext that I will provide employment to some of the people in our new venture. I hope you understand how important this office is for the success of our company. "

This was one thing that Shalini disliked about Paybook. Except for Satvik and Sandeep, almost all the staff was hired by Ashok.

"Ashok, all our employees are good, but we need some diversity. Most of these people are either from your native town or a distant acquaintance of yours. This way, we will promote nepotism in our fledgeling company."

"Shalini, you are putting a false charge on me. I know you are our CEO's wife, but I, Satvik and Sandeep have worked on this idea for last one year. We have brought it to this stage that people are calling it a success. I don't need your unsolicited advice on things that have been working so well," replied Ashok.

"I have also worked in setting up this company. I also deserve equal recognition in the success of this company, not as Satvik's wife but for my own contribution to the company. You are being unfair to me; I will discuss this with Satvik and Sandeep."

Ashok took it as insubordination and a threat to complain against him. He never took indiscipline lightly. He also found Shalini was unnecessarily interfering in his functions.

"Shalini, I am overall responsible for employee function. I was skeptical when Satvik proposed your name in the beginning, but he promised that your role will be limited to product launch and test. I think that phase is over now."

"Are you suggesting that I am no longer required in Paybook?"

"You can make your own decisions," replied Ashok.

Shalini could not tolerate this any further. She walked out of the office in a jiffy. She never realized that her contribution to Paybook would be valued so little.

Satvik was not in the office that day. He had gone for some client meeting. When he returned home, Shalini told him the entire episode.

"I think you and Sandeep are taking a huge risk by giving Ashok a complete free hand in employee functions. He is running this like his party membership. From the security guard to the database administrator, everyone is somehow Ashok's man. Though they are doing a good job, they don't listen to anyone else. At times they point blank refuse my directions and Ashok sides with them."

"I understand your point Shalini, but we have other important things to worry about. We must fix our revenue model, get advertisers and add new features in the product. Sandeep is working on the technology platforms and I am trying to work on the business part. Ashok is managing the logistics and day to day details. If his team is doing their job, we should leave all the hiring and employee functions to Ashok. We have other important things to sort out."

"So, what do you suggest, I leave this job at Paybook?"

"If I were you, I wouldn't. You seem to be genuinely concerned about the well-being of Paybook. If nothing else, you should continue for that reason. You can be instrumental in letting us know if something needs to change."

Shalini was upset at this response but on second thought she realized that Satvik was probably right. If Ashok was making the company more like his political party, it was an even bigger reason that she should counter him not by quitting the company but constantly challenging him.

Satvik met Sandeep over drinks that evening. Though he had dismissed Shalini's observation, he thought of bouncing it off with Sandeep at once.

"Even my technical team has been sourced by Ashok. They have the willingness to learn and work hard but sometimes I don't understand the extra work they do. They stay in the office late along with Ashok. But since they complete their task on time, I don't worry about what else they are doing. Hopefully, they are learning new things with some of the new gadgets I see them using,", replied Sandeep.

"Yes, three of us complimented each other when we set up this company. There are no reasons to believe otherwise. Ashok has been quite committed to the company," Satvik responded.

"Ok, let me show you a great feature that I am working on for our platform. It is one of the latest technological proof of concept that my PhD guide shared with me. It can remotely activate the camera and the voice of the person using this app on any device.

"This can virtually replace phone calls. We will have even more reasons for inviting users to our platform."

"You are the technical brain behind our success Sandeep, we are only trying to sell your idea," replied Satvik.

"The voice and video chat can be activated even today as a user, but it can only be done for your device. If the other person does not allow the connection, it does not happen. In the current feature that I am working on, it does not require the permission from the other person," replied Sandeep.

"This sounds like snooping and we will get into trouble for privacy violation if we even roll out such a feature on Paybook."

"It can be an exclusive service at a premium, and we can limit this feature for very few people. So as far as the privacy violation is in concern, we can add a small clause in our terms and conditions that our users' sign. You can be assured that no one will ever read that," replied Sandeep.

"We definitely need new revenue generation ideas, and this feature could be one of them," Satvik replied.

"If there is someone who would be most interested in a feature like this, it is police and private investigation agencies. It can be helpful in the investigation of crimes and other unlawful activities," said Sandeep.

"If our police ever came to know of a feature like this, they will not only force us to give it to them but to give it to them for free. In fact, we may have to hide it from them. We can explore if we can give it to private investigation agencies. This can also be a double-edged sword, and we need to think more carefully before launching it externally in any form," Satvik replied.

"Here is another idea. I am working on the next wave of social medial – that is called social VR."

"Something like Pokemon Go that was such a craze sometime back. There were millions of downloads of the game.

"Pokemon Go just had one feature, what I am working on is a comprehensive game with thousands of activities like that. One can immerse himself in this world for many days altogether. The only thing he or she needs is food to survive, rest all mental engagement will be taken care of by the virtual reality," replied Sandeep.

"The real life today is very stressful for most people. More people want to escape from reality, where they have little control over things. There are more discontent, angry, and depressed people today in our society than happy and satisfied people. The virtual reality, on the other hand, can be created for the individual whims and fancies. The human mind will probably enjoy it the most."

"Human mind is one of the most interesting subjects of study. It hates the unpleasant situation and implores us to come out of it. However, a prolonged period of pleasure can also make it bored and depressed. So, we must add some challenges in the VR game. The mind will get a kick when it is able to overcome the challenge posed by the game. Understanding of human psychology is the most important thing to make our Paybook successful," Sandeep replied.

Professor's Visit

"Welcome to India Roman, is this your first time?"

Sandeep was looking forward to the visit of his PhD guide from Germany. Even after completing his study, Sandeep had kept in touch with Roman.

"Yes, I am excited to be here, more so after the success of your venture Paybook. India is the happening playground of social media explosion today," replied Roman.

"Thanks for your timely suggestions that helped it grow in user base. But we haven't been able to make it a profitable venture yet. Our friend Satvik is worried about it," replied Sandeep.

"There are many ways to make money. However, what you guys are doing is something exceptional. You have created a giant network where every Indian will be connected. If we can write appropriate algorithms, we will be able to gain remarkable insights that can be easily monetized," Roman replied.

"Look at the sea of people here," he pointed to the crowd at Gateway of India, "If you can control the activity and motivation of each of these people think of the power you will have."

Sandeep never understood the fascination of Roman in this abstract thing called virtual power. Unlike Satvik, he was not interested in making money. His humble lifestyle as a university professor could be the reason behind that but he was no less ambitious.

"I teach students the evolution of human psychology of power and control. That is also an important topic in artificial intelligence today."

"Since the days of cognitive revolution, humans have wondered about the most important question – what is the purpose of their existence? Sooner or later all of us grapple with this question," Said Roman.

"That is called spiritualism in Indian scriptures. Finding out the purpose of self and it's relation with the world," Sandeep replied.

"The very first justification came in the form of religion. It professed that God has a cosmic plan and we all are playing our part in the same. The world is a battleground of good and evil that our soul should navigate through. The religion was a big fiction that helped people to collaborate, create communities and even fight a war. The purpose of life was to live as professed by the scriptures.

"But soon science found that the religion itself is a fiction. The world was not governed by God but by some scientific theories that humans have discovered, and some are yet to be discovered. So, no God could stop the forces of gravity or basic laws of physics. During olden times humans believed that the plague and famines are caused by the curse of God, and there is nothing that can be done about it. With time they discovered that it was our ignorance that was killing people and not any Godly act.

"It was not Gods that created humans but humans that created God to run their own business or to exercise power and control. However, this revelation brought the humans back to square one – what was the purpose of human existence.

"The answer came in as – humanism. Human life is sacred by itself, not because God has created it. The freedom, liberty and human rights are the most important principles around which our world got constructed. The purpose of life was to protect humanity even at the cost of other animals or living beings. Humans replaced God to be at the center of the universe.

"But soon science deflated that bubble as well. It proved that all organisms are nothing but algorithms. Our brain is nothing but a high-powered computer that we are slowly coming to know about and in some cases also exceed it. Till sometime, people believed that human brains had a unique ability to identify human faces that no algorithms can do. Today, it is well proven that Facebook's face recognition program has gone beyond human ability to recognize faces and tag them automatically."

"That is true, every day, we are seeing more and more human exceptionalism being grounded by the power of artificial intelligence. This way, humans will lose their significance once again in the larger scheme of things," asked Sandeep.

"Yes, they will lose significance as a sacred, exceptional, cognitive creature on earth, but they can still retain their relevance by being an important element in the new age religion – Dataism.

"Make no mistake, we are in an era of 'Dataism' – where data is the ultimate truth, the new age God. All of us humans are individual data processors and our value is derived based on how much data we can process. So, the experience is meaningless if it can't be shared. In our daily lives, we read emails, books, articles, poetry etc. process it and produce another set of emails, conversations, articles or images.

"This is the mantra of Gen-X 'record, upload and share'. If you find anything interesting what's the point if you did not record it. If you recorded it, what's the point if you did not upload and share it on social media? We will increasingly consume more data and spit even more data."

"This is a very novel idea, humans as data processors."

"Yes, we are all part of a larger algorithm of an interconnected network that treats each of us as individual chips. We are merely an instrument allowing the free flow of information in this universe."

"We have moved from 'Darwinism' to 'Dataism'."

"Yes, some people believe that this Dataism can solve all our problems in the most scientific way, can take all our decisions most optimally. The algorithm combined with this data can know ourselves more than we do. It may take all the complex decision on our behalf, and we may even be happy about it."

"We can see a good example of that even in the last few years. Now we have given the full authority of defining our route map during travel to Google maps. If there is any conflict between our own view and Goggle, we have started believing the latter already."

"Exactly – and how does the Google map derive its power? Because it can capture and process data much efficiently than our own brains. So, in this digital age data is the key. If you have enough data, you can create an algorithm to control this universe."

"Researchers at the University of Cambridge and Stanford University tested their algorithm on more than 17,000 Facebook users who completed a personality survey and provided the researchers access to their 'likes'. Many of their friends, colleagues and family members also completed the similar test describing the user," Roman said.

"That's really interesting, what was the outcome?"

"The algorithm was able to predict the personality type better than most of the human participants. It needed access to just 10 likes to beat a work colleague, 70 to beat a roommate, 150 to beat a parent or sibling and 300 to beat a spouse," replied Roman.

"Wow, that is quite a revelation. At this rate soon, Facebook will know more about our personality than we know ourselves."

"Yes, then we will eventually ask Facebook – 'Facebook, who should I marry or what kind of job will suit me the most?'" said Roman.

"Facebook will sift through the numerous interactions that we might have had and suggest the most compatible spouse or the best suitable job for us based on our personality types, skills and temperament," Sandeep agreed.

"But I don't see anything wrong with that. If the social media algorithm can predict my compatibility with my prospective spouse, better than myself, I would rather give up my freedom to choose and go by what the algorithm recommends," replied Roman.

"But what happens to privacy, wouldn't people be worried about it?"

"All the noise around privacy is just noise. Don't we share our travel details with Uber for the convenience of finding a cab at the right time?"

"You are right Roman; we are more than willing to share the personal details if we get value out of it. Privacy is just a wishful thinking today," Sandeep replied.

Roman explained this further-

> *"There can be nothing more private than the genetic code we carry, right? I asked during one of my presentations to the audience - how many of you would share your DNA samples if I can offer you free Gene sequencing. It can effectively predict your future health.*
>
> *About 40% of the audience raised their hand. The remaining 60% thought privacy was an issue.*
>
> *When I did a similar survey among millennials – more than 80% agreed to share.*
>
> *The gene sequencing currently costs 1000 dollars, but the price has been coming down consistently. If it really becomes free one day, I don't think anyone will hesitate to share this most personal data.*
>
> *In the digital age, privacy is just wishful thinking because the benefit of sharing data far outweighs privacy concerns.*

"I know a health insurance company that reduces your premium amount if you wear a fit-bit device provided by them. The device will transmit all your private data, including your personal lifestyle habits, e.g. your sleeping time, physical activity, travel, and eating habits. They say these things help them determine the health index of the person, which eventually helps the person in reducing the insurance premium. In case of an emergency like a heart attack, the device can automatically send a signal to the hospitals for someone to help. So, this is a win-win proposition for the company as well as their customer at the cost of their privacy," said Roman.

"But some people may not be willing to trade this breach of privacy with the insurance discount," stated Sandeep.

"As long as it is a personal decision, some people may act that way. But imagine that a large corporation ties up with the insurance company to provide health insurance and improve productivity for their people. The corporation may make it mandatory, or else the employees may have to pay fine.

"You can extend the same logic to the government of any country. They can create a small implantable chip that can be inserted in the human body to track all health parameters. The government may make it mandatory for their people to put on all these snooping gadgets in the name of better medical care. It is a seemingly noble goal to keep everyone happy and hale. It can eventually improve the life expectancy of people using this data."

"Using some artificial intelligence, this trove of data can be used as a weapon by the government against their own citizens. This can eventually lead to an authoritarian government and this is really scary.

"That's why I say that in this age of AI, data privacy is a utopian concept. Knowingly or unknowingly, everyone will agree to share their data for the right benefits.

"Now you understand why I think Paybook can be the next most powerful thing. If we get enough data from the users, our platform will know more about the people than the government. Once we know, we can start controlling the choices they make, we can become the master of their destiny using their data. We can be the next God of social media," concluded Roman.

The busy traffic in Mumbai can be painful. But Sandeep was enjoying the conversation with his professor, someone whom he always respected for his technical knowledge and philosophical interpretation of things.

"I want to use the Paybook data for a social experiment," Ramon told Satvik when they reached the office.

"I think we will have to check on privacy conditions," replied Satvik.

"It is only for academic purposes. We always get data from the industry and share our academic insights with them. It is win-win for both," replied Roman.

Roman explained the ongoing research happening in the field of brain science and artificial intelligence. He talked about several companies that are working in the field of brain-computer interface.

"But how will we benefit from this research?" Satvik asked.

"In the digital world, the winner takes it all. If Paybook can be the first company leveraging this technology, it can acquire unimaginable power over people's lives," replied Roman.

Ashok protested this arrangement but thanks to Sandeep's insistence they agreed that Ramon can use this data for his experiment. Satvik thought they could be up to something unprecedented since the days of Facebook.

A Notification

"Satvik, there is a courier in your name, the courier boy is asking for you specifically," Sandeep walked up to his table and asked him to collect it.

"If it is a company courier, anyone can receive it."

"It seems unusual because it has come by speed post and the delivery boy is insisting on personal receipt."

"Who sends courier by speed post these days, except the government department? Was it some notification from government agencies?" For a moment, Satvik felt a bit worried.

Satvik was right, there was a small brown envelope with the IT ministry seal on it. Satvik opened the letter. It was a typed one, the letter was very brief. It was addressed to Satvik. He was requested to meet the IT minister to discuss the functioning of Paybook and related social media issues. The topic mentioned was very generic. The letter had the contact details of the secretary to fix an appointment.

"Why would the IT ministry summon us, unless they want to interfere in our working? I tell you this government wants to control everything, including social media," said Ashok.

"Or they believe that we are violating some rule," said Sandeep.

"Sandeep and Ashok, I think both of you must come along as well. I have never met these ministry folks. They have not

102

even shared the subject of the discussion clearly. I hope they haven't found something wrong with our company," Satvik said.

"Satvik, they are very specific in who they want to meet and the purpose of the meeting. Since it specifically mentions your name, I think you should call up the IT secretary and fix the appointment as early as possible. And don't worry in case the secretary agrees for us to accompany you, we would come along," replied Ashok calmly.

For the first time, Satvik realized the downside of the CEO role. While Sandeep and Ashok were an equal party, it was Satvik who was answerable to anyone external to the company.

Satvik called the contact number given the next moment

"Sir, this is Satvik Malhotra from Paybook. I have been given this number to fix an appointment with the IT minister."

"Yes, the minister said that the meeting is a bit urgent, so he requested you to come over as soon as possible."

Satvik was worried about the meeting itself, now the word urgent added to his anxiety. He checked the next available flight to Delhi and sought an appointment for the day after in the morning hours.

When he reached home, Satvik was worried.

"Shalini, I have never met these ministry people, I am not sure what they are going to ask."

"Social media is a new thing for everyone, the government people hardly even understand the way it works. He must have called you to take some opinions around some new policies they might be formulating. They might be hoping to understand this from you."

What Shalini said possibly made sense but Satvik kept thinking about this meeting. He could not sleep well that night. He wanted to get over with the meeting somehow. He was in Delhi early morning pretty much before time.

The government offices have not changed one of the reasons could be that they are still housed in heritage buildings with unchanged settings from the pre-internet era. The structure was overwhelming for Satvik.

Satvik was greeted by the secretary, a short height man who introduced himself as Sarvesh. After waiting for some 30 minutes, he accompanied him into the IT minister's office. It was a spacious room with colossal wooden structures and sofas. A small Indian flag replica was prominently displayed on the table. There was a bundle of files stacked on the table. The room was full of paper files while a chart proudly displayed the government commitment to make the office paperless.

Satvik sat on one of the sofas, waiting anxiously for the reason he was summoned to Delhi. The minister kept signing the files for a few minutes before he asked Satvik.

"Mr. Satvik, your company Paybook has grown very popular in India. Everyone is talking about it. Our government is very supportive of entrepreneurship and we wish you good success in that."

Satvik guessed that something ominous might be coming after the pause.

"But we are also aware of the misuse of social media for political purposes. As you know, considering the general election, we have to make sure that these tools are not used to subvert our democratic objectives."

"Sir, I did not understand. How our small social media company can interfere with the election process of such a

104

large country? Moreover, we do not create content, people share whatever post they want, and we don't even sensor that," Satvik responded incredulously.

"You may not be creating the content, but you must be aware that fake news is really impacting our democratic process. I am told that there is propaganda material created by unknown sources that sometimes instill fear and create panic among people. I am not asking you to stop criticizing government policies or whatever. Still, if fake news and propaganda material are being publicized on your platform, you will have to control the same. You can't feign ignorance that you are not a media company and hence should not be regulated. We are working on a framework to control this menace. For the time being, you will have to demonstrate that you are taking effective steps to control the same. Hope you will abide by the government submission and send us a report in one-month time."

"Sir, what specifically you want me to address in the report?"

"If there are propaganda material shared on your platform that is likely to be false, you have to report the same to us and share details of the post creator."

"But how would we know if a particular criticism is false or a fake item. People share all kind of opinions and views, none of us can verify that it is not possible."

"See, newspapers publish a lot of news items every day, but they still can't get away if they publish a fake item."

Satvik got the message, there was not much point in arguing with the minister. He was indirectly saying that excessive targeting of his government may affect their election prospects, and hence such contents must be censored. The minister had a little problem with the fake news that supported the current government policies and achievements.

"Sir, I understand the concern, and we are committed to abiding by your recommendation. I will soon get back to you on this," Satvik got the message in this brief meeting.

'I would have to take some tangible actions and produce a compliance report,' he thought. When he reached Mumbai Sandeep and Ashok were equally curious to know.

Satvik set up a meeting with the entire team. Mostly the company discussions used to take place informally, but this was a serious matter and needed some focused problem-solving.

"Ashok, the minister is essentially saying that our platform is being used for spreading fake news and misinformation against his government," Satvik said.

"He would have meant that slowly Paybook is becoming an awareness tool for the common citizens, and it is exposing government propaganda. Our platform is free and based on the principles of freedom of expression. We do not want to sanction any post even if it is highly critical of the government policies. Like all media companies, we have setup Paybook on liberal values. I feared the government meddling as our platform is being endorsed as a tool for public expression. In essence, it will eventually bring the revolution that we all need in our society," Ashok gave a long reply and kind of dismissed the concern raised by Satvik.

"I have also read various reports that our platform is becoming a propaganda tool for radical left ideologies," Sandeep responded.

This pretty much angered Ashok, as it was a direct accusation on him to sabotage the social media platform.

"Look guys, I belong to the communist party, and it should not be a surprise to you. This office space is essentially our party office. I got this space on the condition that it would employ some of our party workers as well. Many of the current employees who have worked hard to make Paybook a successful company are our party members. We can't take it away from them. And yes, we all have ideologies, and we should not be shy of expressing ourselves. The minister was worried about his own party's defeat and he was trying to arm-twist us. We need not censor any post at all," replied Ashok.

"Ashok, your party has to fight the electoral battle and register the win there. Our company can't be the battlefield for the same. We all will get badly impacted if we allow this to happen," Sandeep said.

"The electoral battle is not only fought on the day of voting in the polling booth. It must be approached from various angles, one of them is media activism. We need intellectual voices to bring out the disparity in society. And those voices should be fearless and loud," replied Ashok.

"Do you think Paybook will really bring the revolution that you believe in?"

"Yes, why not, one day it will bring the revolution if we stay the course and resist any attempt of government meddling."

Now Satvik understood why Ashok insisted that all hiring should only be done through him. He recalled the resistance that Shalini faced when she recommended some of her colleagues. Everyone knew that Ashok had radical left ideologies since college days, he believed in some utopian Marxist revolution that would remove the class differences and solve all problems. Satvik thought with time Ashok would have tempered down and adopted a more mature approach.

For Satvik, the minister's words were still very clear in his mind. It was a soft warning that some of the unsubstantiated propaganda items need to be moderated. He clearly called out how the fake posts by motivated agencies can jeopardize the free elections. Allegedly, it was an issue in the American election so it can't be dismissed entirely. But here Ashok was adamant about staying the course. Satvik was wondering whether it was easier to confront Ashok or the minister. Ashok wielded disproportionate power in company affairs. He ran the entire operation. He provided the office space, and almost all the employees came from his acquaintances and party workers. Confronting him meant that he could just fire Satvik and continue Paybook as usual. For Ashok, Paybook was a party mission, he would never abandon that. Satvik thought not to disrupt the current situation.

"I think if it continues like this, you will soon be in trouble," Shalini told Satvik. She was never too comfortable with the excessive control that Ashok had in company affair.

"I know Shalini, I am wondering if I can still convince the minister by saying that we have set up an audit team that would keep an eye on any reported violation of Paybook policies," replied Satvik.

"And that audit team will report to Ashok, right?"

"Sometimes you have to do monkey balancing," Satvik knew that he was postponing the problem for a future date.

108

Holiday Trip

The hectic work schedule was taking its toll on Satvik. That is why he was looking forward to this family holiday break. He had planned to go to Ooty, a hill station in southern India. It was a nice escape from the heat and sweat of Mumbai.

The six-hour drive from Bangalore to Ooty was quite good. It passed through the Mysore city and Bandipur National park. Satvik knew that his son Akash will enjoy this experience of spotting the wild animals in the most natural setup. As a kid, he himself recalled going to the zoo and having fun with his father.

"See those herd of deer Akash, you must have seen them only in pictures, here you see how they look," Satvik told his son.

Akash looked outside the window for a few minutes and then switched back to his phone. He was not at all amused by the sight of various animals, as if they could not his divert his attention from his phone. Satvik thought he was playing some video game. Suddenly his eyes caught something familiar – Paybook. Satvik was surprised and even worried that his twelve-year-old son was already using the social media app.

"Akash – Paybook app is only for adults who are 18 years and above. How can you be on social media at such a tender age?"

"Most of my friends in school use this app, Papa. It is fun. The age check just asks for our date of birth, we give an earlier date to bypass that.

"But what exactly you and your friends do there?"

"It is quite interesting. My friends and I post nice pictures – based on the likes and comments on that we get some credits of money. They say it is virtual money, but it can be used to purchase things. One of my friends has earned enough points to credit him one thousand rupees. With this money, he has planned to buy other video games after a year. We have a competition among our friends – to earn the maximum money."

Satvik recalled the pebble game that Ashok was talking about. These were virtual pebbles that the current young generation was playing. He was getting alarmed at every new sentence that he was hearing from his son.

"Shalini, I am not sure if it is true, but it seems Steve Jobs never gave the iPhone and iPad to his own kids. Because he was aware of the bad influence the devices can have on the development of a child. They can be addictive; they can hamper the healthy development and growth."

"It is a surprise to me as much as it is to you. Akash has been spending a lot of time on my phone, but I thought it was only for playing video games and other games kids play. But looks like he has created a profile on Paybook and is using it as an adult member. It seems it is already a craze among his school friends which is even more worrying. The anonymity with the bitcoin makes it difficult even to track who is transacting, leave aside any age checks," replied Shalini.

"Did I ever tell you the story about Ramesh, who we met on Goa beach one day? He had a young kid like ours, who was spending a lot of time online. He fell in the trap of a weird 'Blue Whale' game and eventually committed suicide. The parents had no clue about it. Social media is one of the most dangerous platforms for the impressionable mind. Delete his profile from Paybook and stop him from using the mobile phone."

"These knee jerk reactions would not solve the problem Satvik. You heard, he said that many of his friends are on this platform and they are already addicted to it. Even if we delete his profile, he will find some workaround to circumvent that."

"We never really thought about the kids and the impact on them when we conceptualized this app. It is coming back to haunt us. But we need to do something about it. Let me speak to Sandeep on adding extra security checks that will flush out all the underage users of the platform," Satvik told Shalini.

All through the vacation, this thought kept playing in Satvik's mind. The downhill drive in the taxi was very scenic.

"This route has 36 hair pin bends and possibly one of the most dangerous one in the country. Every day there are accidents due to brake failure and skidding. There is a longer route with a relatively flat and less dangerous road, but most people prefer this as it has a much better view," the driver explained.

"Your job as a taxi driver is so dangerous, you are really a courageous person to do it for your living," replied Satvik.

"Thank you, may I ask what you do?"

"I am the head of a company called Paybook, have you heard about it?"

"Paybook – it is very popular in our city as well, one of my friends says one can use it to generate easy money as well as have a lot of fun. He was telling me it is better than driving taxi all day. But I don't understand one thing if everyone is getting paid for just browsing, clicking and writing comments who is actually paying for all this?" the driver asked inquisitively.

"It is very simple, each one of us generates a large amount of data in our digital footprint on social media. This data is of huge interest to product marketers. We share that data for a price and share the revenue with the users who are the source of the data. Secondly, since we have a lot of users online, the advertisers pay us. So, it is a win-win arrangement for the users as well as the product marketers," explained Satvik.

"I think what you say makes sense, Sir. I thought it could well turn out to be a Ponzi scheme that we hear every other day. No wonder your product is getting so popular every day. I will also learn how to earn money by using the same."

Satvik was very flattered hearing that Paybook was getting adoption in every nook and the corner in the country. 'I should just fix the unintended use by minors like my son,' he thought. On returning to the office, he met Sandeep and explained the entire problem.

"I can't think of any foolproof technical solution. If a child has access to the internet and has learned about this application from his friends, he will eventually do it. Add on top of it the lure of earning money by easy clicks, young kids can easily get swayed by it."

"How about we add some more questions like graduation date check or one-time password sent to the phone or any biometric details?"

"Our login process has to be user friendly, if we try to add a lot of questions and inconvenience, it will impact our future enrollments. Moreover, whatever we do, the kids will find a solution to break through it. The only foolproof option could be if we use the Aadhar number to validate the actual date of birth. But you know the issue with such an approach today," replied Sandeep.

"People are very skeptical of misuse of personal data, why would the government ever share the same with us. This will also be a suicidal action for our company," replied Satvik.

"Do you have any idea of how many underage kids could be part of our Paybook profile database?"

"Your guess could be as good as mine, I have no idea at all," replied Sandeep.

Satvik asked the school principal in the next parents-teacher meet - "Is the cellphone usage by kids a real problem?"

"It is not only a real problem but reaching a clinical level today. The younger kids are twice as vulnerable to the radio frequency (RF) waves due to thin skull and bones. There was a study by the American Medical Association that indicated that this excessive radiation of RF waves could possibly lead to some form of brain cancer. Only the time will tell the effect of the long-term radiation on kids. We were lucky in a way that the cellphones were invented when we were already adult. Imagine the effect of the same on a child that starts using phones from as early as 8 years today.

"Many countries are waking up to the ill effects of cell phones, especially on the kids. You would be surprised to know that some countries like the UK already have smartphone rehab centers for kids as young as 13 years old. In Russia, scientists and government officials have advised that anyone under the age of 18 years should not use cell phones. In France, marketing of cell phones towards kids is banned.

"As per one Indian study, cell phone users who were on the phone for sixty minutes a day over four years experienced damage to the DNA in roughly 40 percent of their cells. The main issue with the cell phones is the microwave radiation, especially within the distance of six inches, farther the device from the brain the safer it is. You can imagine the impact of standing near a microwave oven all day, the radiation can impact various tissues and cells."

"I thought the cellphone usage was only impacting the behavioral aspects like lack of concentration, diminishing social skills and increased anxiety, leading to mental health concerns. I am aware of some of the dangerous games like Blue Whale that target vulnerable kids. What you are describing is the biological ill effects on brain and DNA leading to dangerous disease. It is really alarming how we are still ignorant of the same. How can we control this in the kids?" Satvik said.

"We have hired psychologists in the school who specialize in the smartphone addiction of the kids. Most of the parents do not realize that the kids learn from their own behavior. If they want to control the cellphone usage of their child, they will have to resist their own temptation to be on social media every waking hour," replied the principal.

Satvik was intrigued by this conversation. He did some google search that day and discovered that whatever the Principal was saying was probably right. The radiation coming out of any electronic device can be dangerous to humans. The wireless and cordless phones have added to this problem even more. But this was the time to fix this, starting with his own behavior from now on.

Satvik stopped using his phone as the alarm clock, he switched over to earplugs while talking so that he would keep the phone away from his brain as much as possible. Sometimes at night, he would switch off the power supply of his bedroom so that all electronic devices were deactivated.

"You are over correcting yourself. You can't cut off cell phones and social media from our lives today. It has become as essential as water and food," Shalini cautioned Satvik.

"I have to be a role model myself before I insist on Akash to control his mobile phone addiction. The kids learn from their parents by observing what they do and not what they are told."

Problems

It has been one and a half year since the creation of Paybook. Satvik and Sandeep have provided some 50 lakhs rupees which were used up in setting up the company and operational expenses. Incidentally, there was minimal cost in an office setup, and employee wages were insignificant as it was managed by Ashok for free.

For Satvik the idea of setting this company was to make good money and not run like a small business. He was, however, running out of ideas on how to generate good revenue from this. The lock-in period of two years was also approaching. Sandeep estimated that even if 10% of people plan to cash out their Paybook points, it may well be beyond 5 crores. Something had to be done quickly to arrange for the funds.

"Why not we meet some venture capitalists, they may fund for the next level expansion of Paybook," Sandeep suggested Satvik.

"I always thought that most of these startup events are like song and dance. But we do need external fund, we will have to pitch it to some of the investors and see how this idea is received."

Both Sandeep and Satvik set up a meeting with Anand, a partner from Digital Ventures, a private equity firm that was investing in the new age ideas like this.

"I think your idea is catchy. But you must understand that investors like us invest only in profitable business. We want to first understand how much economic potential it has. What is your revenue model?" asked Anand.

"When we started this company, our idea was that people and businesses will pay for advertising on this platform. We planned to share with them the data of customers that could be used to target the right segment for businesses. This, we thought, was the most direct way to reach the customer. This revenue we thought could partly be shared with the customers as Paybook points for their engagement on the platform," said Satvik.

"We thought, the companies will jump at an idea like this. However, our earnings from advertisements have been hardly anything. On the other hand, we need to pay the customers when they cash out their loyalty point in six months times. We are burning money every day. The amount was small earlier, but with the increasing customer base, we could soon be bankrupt," added Sandeep.

"What are the other ways to make money? You have a large user base and growing, can you add a small fee, and will they pay?" Anand asked.

"No, not at all. Our platform promised to be a revenue generation means for our customer. There is no way that we can charge money from them. Our users come to our platform to earn money but not to pay. Moreover, social media has become more like emails today, no one believes that it can be a paid service," replied Satvik.

"Our only asset is data; we have collected a huge amount of behavioral data of our users. We also have the users' consent to share this data with the advertisers. If this data can be monetized, we can make a lot of money. That can be our business model," added Sandeep.

"Selling of private data for various purposes is a very controversial topic these days. Though there are not enough laws in India, stringent laws are coming up in some of the European countries and the US. India will soon follow. This will make any personal data misuse a grave offence. Hence this will be a risky business and no external investor like us would ever invest in the same," Anand replied.

"The problem with Paybook is not that it is burning money at a fast rate, a lot of business are cash negative but still are able to raise good funds. To convince investors, you need a good story. Currently, Paybook lacks a clear goal and direction," Anand added further.

This essentially meant that it would be difficult for Paybook to arrange for any external funding. Satvik was worried before meeting Anand, he got even more worried with what Anand shared. In any business, an increase in user base is a healthy sign, but here Satvik was more worried as it increased his financial burnout. At this rate, Satvik would soon turn bankrupt. The idea that he thought would make him a millionaire was stripping him of whatever wealth he already had.

"These days lot of startups look for funding from the public, why can't we explore such an option," Shalini told Satvik.

"That is called crowd-funding. You will find some of them even in this newspaper," Satvik turned over the newspaper and pointed to the startup segment.

Shalini looked at the section curiously, "Isn't it funny that we are paying one set of users by the funds provided by another set of people."

"This is what business is all about in most simple terms," replied Satvik.

"Wait, it looks like someone has already advertised for Paybook."

"What are you saying?" Satvik looked at the advertisement closely. Shalini was right. He read it aloud.

To all our users of Paybook

We at Paybook are two-year-old today. During this time, our user base has grown from zero to 20 million. This amazing achievement has been possible only due to unflinching love from all of you. It has also provided financial benefits to some of you, however small it may be. We will continue to serve you through this endeavor.

Today, however, we need a small support from all of you. We request you all to withhold your encashment of paybook points for next one year. We will need this time to resolve some internal payment issues before we are back with our usual program. We want to categorically deny some of the rumors that Paybook is any kind of Ponzi scheme.

From

Paybook Management team

"Looks like Ashok read your mind and gave this advertisement," Shalini said.

"No, this is committing suicide for a business like ours."

Shalini did not quite understand what Satvik was trying to say. But before she could ask anything more, Satvik rushed to his room to pick up his phone and called Sandeep.

"Did Ashok discuss with you before putting the advertisement in the newspaper?"

"I am not even aware that there was anything like that. But I was getting alarmed at increased cash out options from many of Paybook users," replied Sandeep.

"This will create panic among users. This is exactly what one should not do in a crisis like this. We are dead now," said Satvik.

"We must meet Ashok now and find out why he did so."

In the office, Ashok was unaware of the havoc he had caused in just a few hours of the advertisement.

"Users are part of the Paybook community, I am sure they would support us in the time of crisis. That is why I was transparent with them to share the current state of affair," Ashok tried to defend.

"Today's digital users are not like factory workers of the last generation who would forgo their remuneration for a few months if there was a financial crisis. If they suspect there could be a financial crisis, they would withdraw their own part and disappear," Satvik scolded Ashok.

"Ashok, Satvik is right. The meteoric rise of digital companies today is also followed by a crash due to one foolish step. Word of mouth will spread like wildfire."

"I am really sorry for this oversight. How can we contain this crisis now?"

"There is only one option, don't block any encashment. We need to understand the user psychology."

"But there is an increased demand for encashment from our platform. Almost every user is cashing the loyalty point. We have a huge user base; we will have to wind up if this continues even for a few days like this. Our cash reserves are almost dry," Sandeep explained in short.

"It is like 'run to the bank' that happens sometimes. When the customers believe that the bank is going down, everyone tries to withdraw, and even though the bank finances are good, it can become bankrupt due to this frenzy. Can we limit or partially block this feature for only a few days?" Satvik asked.

"That will further erode the little confidence that the users may have. We need to arrange for some short-term financer," implored Sandeep.

"I have bad news on finances. The investor who we were banking on heavily to invest in our company, has backed out saying we do not have a sustainable business model. According to him our greatest asset, data will soon be subject to several government laws, and we will not be able to sell that legally," replied Satvik.

"We need to salvage ourselves. Can we sell our company and make money out of it, we have created a good brand value?"

"It will be a fire sale. They will ask the similar question that Anand was asking. How much money we are making in this venture? I find it weird, but at this stage, we may have to even pay to sell our company. Sometimes I feel it was a bad decision to start this company, we did not think through. Last one year we have only lost our savings," Satvik replied.

Satvik realized that he had to quickly do something to arrange for the finances. He could not sleep well that night. In his dream, he was being chased by the thousands of people who wanted their money back. They were angry, and some even had stones in their hand. Satvik stopped for a while and argued with one of them

"Why are you upset about it so much, you did not invest any money? I have not stolen your money that you are so angry."

"It is my money, in a way. Paybook promised to pay me three thousand rupees and it was this money I was banking on for my future expenses. You have to return our money," responded the angry man who was followed by several others.

Satvik realized the issue was in creating the expectation. But how will he handle the mass hysteria? He woke up suddenly and was relieved that it was only a bad dream. But he had to find a solution soon enough.

"Is there any way we can generate money from Paybook?" Satvik asked Sandeep.

"There are a few analytics companies which can be interested in our user-based data. One of them is a political research company from China. They met us last month and were quite keen that we share our database with them," Sandeep asked.

"How can a political research organization make use of our data?"

"Well, they say they have an established methodology, and they have worked with other social media startups. They analyze the comments and likes of the users. Based on the last few interactions on social media, they can profile the users and identify their personal and political preferences. This data they pass on to their campaign department who carefully design advertisements to influence the political choices. For example, if the user is a single mother, there is a specific type of advertisements created and shown on her feed that she could be interested in. This can be so targeted that a very personalized political campaign can be run," replied Sandeep.

"And who pays for these advertisements?" asked Satvik.

"It is all political expense, and you know where the election funds come from," replied Sandeep.

"Such kind of one-on-one targeted campaign can infringe on the democratic process. Someone who has this large pool of data can slowly brainwash the users into believing any political ideology. Is this what the minister was referring to?" recalled Satvik.

"This is exactly what Ashok's party is trying to use this platform for as well. I have seen that his communist party leaders direct him with very specific goals. They have a count of people in each area, each street. It is very easy to find that from the address and location details in our application. Then he categorizes them as a loyal supporter, sympathizer, indifferent, opposition and staunch opposition. He combines this data with personal demographics and creates a targeted campaign for each demographic and category combination.

"He tracks this data on a week to week basis that tells him how effective his campaigns have been in converting the naysayers into his party supporters. This process is very precise and effective. The user is not aware that the contents have been highly tailored to influence his political preferences. There are even more alternate ways where some bots can be created using artificial intelligence. They can create content (or morph from the news links) exactly what a certain type of user would like. These bots can first read from the user behavior and reinforce them by feeding more of similar contents. The best thing is that the user may not even know that he is following a bot who is influencing his thoughts and actions," replied Sandeep.

"Now I understand why Ashok's party was willing to provide his office space for our work, it is the most effective ideological canvassing, better than any door to door campaign," replied Satvik

"If you think carefully, we are sitting on a gold mine of data. We just need to find out the right set of people who could be interested in this data. Some of them are willing to pay many times more than what Anand could have financed. My PhD professor guide in Germany says that even a lot of international agencies could be interested in our database. But we must be careful that the data does not land up in the hands of bad elements else it can be used as a weapon," Sandeep replied.

"This is not the time that we can worry about morality or personal privacy. If someone is willing to pay for our data, I am more than willing to sell the same. What was the name of the company that you said were interested in Paybook data?" asked Satvik.

"They operate under different names in different countries. In India, they have a local arm. They are not publicly listed, more like a consulting setup to different political parties?"

"And how much are they willing to pay?"

"Well, much more than what we need to tide over our current crisis."

"We don't have a choice, who knows this could eventually be the best business model that we could ever think of," replied Satvik.

"But elections will soon be over, and this type of funding will dry up. Last week we had an agency from Russia that approached us for the data access. They were willing to pay two million dollars per year for a five-year contract. Ramon introduced them to me. But they want more than the data," replied Sandeep.

"That's like a gold mine. What did they want?"

"I don't know about their business, but they said they had a worldwide network and were looking for an agency in India. They wanted complete access to our platform to identify the right customers for their products. They were not forthcoming on talking about the product or algorithm they plan to use. But I wonder what kind of business makes it possible for them to pay us two million dollars a year," explained Sandeep.

"There are different types of businesses people do over the world, we need not worry about them. We must run our own business and we need money to do that. I don't think we will be violating any laws by collaborating with them. If we are funded well, we will serve our customers better. If we have enough money, we can even fight the court cases. It is all in the interest of our customers," Satvik explained.

"Shall I call them next week?

"Yes, let us proceed with the deal."

Satvik was relaxed for the time being. Shalini and Sandeep cautioned him that they were pushing the boundary too far, but Satvik was already feeling the heat of running a cash strapped business, he had to push the boundaries somehow.

More Troubles

It was a Sunday morning. For Satvik it was the only day when he could wake up late, rest all days he would leave for the office latest by 8 am. He was planning to go out and spend the early morning leisurely in the nearby park. He had not been there since quite some time. His son, Akash especially enjoyed the open lakeside view in the park. The lake was renovated recently, and the clean water attracted different varieties of birds. The lake also had a beautiful jogging track.

'I too should start jogging,' Satvik thought. His health was taking a beating in the last few months, thanks to worries about Paybook.

His cell phone rang. 'I would not take any calls today,' he thought. But the phone rang again after two minutes and then again. Satvik picked up the third time.

"Sir, there is a police team at our office, they want you here," the office boy was getting panicked.

"Why are they there, and what are they asking?"

"I don't know, sir they are asking you to come over to the office. They say if you don't come in the next two hours, they might even break open the door."

Now Satvik got worried. Why a police team would come to his small office on Sunday afternoon? It did not seem like a small thing. He told Shalini that there was some emergency at the office, and he would be back by the afternoon as they had planned to go out late evening for dinner.

While driving his way to the office Satvik thought, was this, in any way, connected with the laptop theft they had last week? He was telling Sandeep not to lodge police complaint as it could unnecessarily complicate the matter. But Sandeep was insistent that not complaining would encourage the thief to repeat the act, especially if it was someone internal in the office. On second thought he suspected it could be related to the IT minister meeting as he had still not submitted the report after asking for a few extensions. On a few occasions, there were police complaints by some people on some of the social media posts. These complaints usually needed the details of the Paybook user data. They were kind of nuisance but unavoidable in this business.

Being Sunday, it took Satvik far lesser time to reach the office, but to him, it felt far too long than usual. His mind was racing faster than his car until he reached his office.

There was a police jeep parked near the gate. There were 3 policemen waiting at the entrance of the office, but unlike the usual khaki dress, they were wearing a black sweatshirt with NIA written in bold letters. Satvik had seen such visuals in movies only, it increased his heart rate even more.

Satvik greeted them first, introduced himself before asking the guard to open the office premises.

"Is there anything serious?" asked Satvik, looking at one of the persons.

"Yes, it is. You must have read that last week ten of our CRPF jawans were martyred due to an attack by Naxalites in Andhra?"

Satvik had read about the horrible news. Last few days the TV anchors were shouting at the top of their voice that it was an attack on the country. Some said it was not possible without the active collaboration from some insiders. These conspiracy theories were good to watch from the comfort of the drawing room. Here at office, Satvik did not even want to think about them.

"Do you recognize this person?" the inspector flashed a passport-sized photograph to Satvik.

"No," nodded Satvik.

"Ok what about this one?"

It was a group photo of several men surrounding a woman who appeared like teaching them something. One of the persons looked like the one from the previous photograph. But Satvik recognized the lady easily.

"The lady in the picture is Beny, who is one of our part-time employees. She visits our office occasionally, but I have met her only once or twice. Ashok deals with her more often," replied Satvik.

"And let me tell you, that the man on the left side of the lady is identified as one of the commanders of the Naxal group, now killed in last week's incident. We have recovered his body," inspector's voice turned harsh at this point.

At this point, Satvik was at his wit's end. He could not say anything for the next few minutes. The inspector was trying to insinuate something.

"Beny is a reputed professor and a charity worker."

"That is her day job. She has also been helping these Naxal groups in recruiting and getting funding from foreign sources. We have found traces of connections leading to her for few past terror activities as well."

"We have strong information that your social media platform is being used for many anti-national activities, and some of your employees are complicit in the same," the inspector said in no uncertain terms.

"If you have this evidence you can question Beny, but I don't think we should be held responsible for the action of lakhs of Paybook users."

Satvik added further, "Just like a telephone and internet is used by all kind of people, Paybook has different types of users. Some of the users might be involved in undesirable activities, we have no way to know that beforehand. We extend full support to police during any investigation whenever they request. We don't encourage any illegal activities; our employees are law-abiding citizens. Paybook is only a platform for communication," replied Satvik.

"Our preliminary investigation reveals that your platform is being used for illegal activities. Many of these criminals and terrorists now know that the common medium like phone and emails are under surveillance but the social media like yours is still not under check. More importantly, we believe that many of your employees are part of the underground network," replied the inspector.

"How can you create a malicious charge like this, what evidence do you have?"

The inspector pulled out a file that had printouts of many pages of Paybook message feeds. He handed over one of the sheets to Satvik.

"I can't understand what is written. Sometimes the users communicate using emojis and sign languages that create junk messages. I think they result from the word processing errors by our platform. We are trying to fix the same," replied Satvik.

"Mr. Satvik they are not garbage signs, they are some code words that these people use to avoid any oversight. We have decoded some of these messages, and it is quite alarming that your platform has become the first choice for terrorist elements."

Satvik looked at the printouts, they looked genuine screenshots of Paybook application. By this time Sandeep had also reached the office.

"Sandeep, can we find these messages in our database?"

Sandeep searched through the database for a few minutes. Those messages could not be found.

"These criminals are smarter than most of you. On top of your platform, some of these users have created a messaging system where the messages can be self-destroyed once the intended user has seen the same. That is why you can't find those messages in your system anymore," explained the inspector.

Satvik and Sandeep were surprised and shocked at this discovery. Sandeep was planning to work on such a feature to avoid increasing data load on Paybook. However, it was low on his priority list as he thought not many users would really want a feature like this. Here the inspector was telling him that someone had already built this feature on top of his platform and was using it successfully even without his knowledge. They were scared at this discovery, but Satvik was more worried about getting rid of the inspector.

"Sir, we can share the communication archive of any individual or set of individuals as required by the law," replied Satvik.

While he said that, he thought it was a dangerous idea for his business. If by any chance, his users get to know that their private communication and data is being shared with the police, they will exit from the platform. However, this was the time when Satvik had to think of saving himself, the business could be saved later.

"I hope you will keep this investigation confidential until you really find anything conclusive. If it goes to the media, we will be devastated. We are always more than willing to co-operate with the investigating agencies," Satvik looked for reassurance from the inspector.

"Thanks for the offer. I am sure that you would co-operate. I don't know if you noticed, one of the participants in the secret messaging is your friend Ashok. They are planning other terror incidents including a bomb blast during the Independence Day celebration," the inspector replied.

"What?" - Satvik asked in disbelief - "Ashok can never be engaged in any terrorist activity like this. Why would he do anything like that?"

"Because he is a member of the banned Naxal group. He is an overground cadre who acts as the extended arm of their underground network. We have also found some proof that he has been involved in a few other unlawful activities."

Now Satvik was worried. Shalini had warned him about the secretive behavior of Ashok. Even Sandeep had suspected something fishy but kept quiet as Satvik had dismissed them. Was it a mistake to give Ashok so much freedom to operate?

'Did this mean that Paybook was already weaponized and I will be held responsible for all this? Will I have to go to jail? But why should I be punished for something that Ashok and Beny have allegedly done?' Satvik thought.

"If you have found some evidence, why don't you arrest them and punish them as per the law of the land. We are ready to co-operate with you."

131

"I have enough evidence to arrest Ashok and Benny. However, this is not why I have come here. I could have sent one of my junior staff to get this done," said the inspector further.

"I believe they are part of a larger network and arresting them will alert everybody. We will never be able to catch them in that case. I want to set up a larger net that can nab the entire module."

"I want to check certain things about the technical capability of your platform. Can it enable the video and microphone of the users without the users being aware of it?" the inspector added.

"Technically, it is possible. We can activate the audio and video of the user as soon as he or she has logged into Paybook. Most of the users remain logged in. The video feed can be stored in our servers. I had thought of something like this earlier but then realized that it is an unethical form of snooping. The moment users get to know about it, they will abandon our platform and we will be in legal trouble as well," replied Sandeep.

"We don't have to tell anyone about it," said the inspector.

"Will we not be violating the law by doing something like this, I don't think it is even morally right," replied Satvik.

"Mr. Satvik, the law of the land is silent about this and we should be aware that when it comes to national security, larger good should take the precedence. If we can stop a terrorist attack by violating the privacy rights of a limited number of citizens, it is still a noble cause," replied the inspector.

Now the dilemma was apparent to Satvik and Sandeep. Paybook had already become a double-edged sword, open to misuse by the law breakers as well as law enforcers. This was akin to a dystopian scenario where the autocratic state uses snooping technology on top of the comprehensive data store to virtually control the lives of every citizen. The state knows everything about her citizen and slowly starts manipulating their choices, presumably to keep them safe. This eventually leads to a totalitarian government that can never be dislodged. Satvik was able to relate to the power of centralized data store like Paybook.

"Sir, we understand what you are asking for. Being a small company, we are not quite sure of the legality of the same. These days freedom of expression for the citizens is quite a controversial discussion point. Please give us some time to get back to you. Meanwhile, we can share with you the specific data that you require," that was the politest way Satvik could defer the inspector's request to stealthily activate the phone and camera features for Paybook users.

"In these cases, we don't have time, if something untoward happens it will be disastrous," said the inspector.

"What do you want now?"

"From now onward, the entire database of your solution will be managed by our technical staff with dual password control," replied the inspector.

"We will also activate the phone and microphone of the users as we deem necessary," he added further.

"This is patently wrong. We can't snoop on our own people at your whims and fancies. What if the government uses this data for the upcoming election manipulation?" Satvik asked.

"That will still be less of an issue than a possible terror attack," the inspector was unperturbed.

"See, you have some proof about Ashok and Beny. You can as well arrest them and take control of our platform. You can run with it," Satvik thought with that will also go away the worry of paying the users.

"Just like you, we don't want to create a media spectacle. I don't want to arrest Ashok or Beny at this stage though they would be under our strict surveillance. We also know that you must pay money to users. We don't want to take that obligation," the inspector said.

"We are not going to abide by this. I will raise this with the IT minister – I have to send a report he has asked for, and I am scheduled to meet him next week," Satvik replied.

"I showed you proof against Beny and Ashok. We also have some report that a Russian cartel is selling drugs through Paybook. It seems you signed the contract with them knowing well that it could be unlawful."

"Now you are trying to blackmail us."

"You can call it whatever, but I will come back by the evening. Hopefully, by then you would have made the decision," the inspector left with the ominous warning.

The impact of this discussion was slowly dawning upon Satvik. He was not only implicated but made an unwilling partner in something that he believed, was invariably wrong. He was also running out of money as the Russian contract now would not get signed. Proceeding with that after the warning from the inspector would be suicidal for sure.

"We are in big soup now, Sandeep. This police team will keep a tab on everything we do," told Satvik after the inspector left the office.

"He virtually wants to run his police department using the surveillance data that he may acquire from Paybook. If we deny him the same, he will take it as our refusal to co-operate with the Police. He has already given a stern warning, so we do not have an option now," said Sandeep.

"The users are blaming us that we are cheating them of their rightful money. The minister believes we deliberately create fake news to target their government, and now the Police also think that our platform is being used for some terror activities. We have been hit by problems from everywhere without any single solution in sight. We don't have any investor to back our venture. The way it looks now our company may go bust, and all of us may land in jail soon. The police already have enough ground to do the same. We are in terrible soup Sandeep, and I can't think of any practical solution. I am afraid to even break this news to Shalini," said Satvik.

"I see a silver lining in this."

"What are you saying?" asked Satvik.

"Yes, all this while if there was one person who consistently blocked our ideas, it was Ashok. We were dependent on him as he provided key resources for the company. I had a suspicion that he was using this platform for some vested purpose, the police inquiry only proved that right. Now I can relate why he was insistent on hiring a certain type of people only. We can fire him now and start the clean-up process," replied Sandeep.

"With him gone we will have a genuine opportunity to rediscover our company and define its new purpose," he added further.

"But we don't have any good idea to salvage our situation."

"It has been too much to handle for us. We need some time off from all this nonsense," said Satvik.

"Let us go back to the place where we got this inspiration. Remember we met Ramesh there and he had some really great suggestion for us. His life was completely spoiled, just as we feel now, and he was able to claim it back. We are in a similar situation today. We need external advice, someone who can look at our situation more dispassionately," replied Sandeep.

"Yes, I recall. He did not only recover from the mishap but also set up a different type of setup that was doing exceedingly well. Maybe we can look for inspiration on how to run a company in this social media world. He also offered to help us with our venture at that time."

"We need a break anyway to secure our peace of mind. My head is spinning already," said Satvik.

Mindfulness

Satvik had noted the address of Ramesh's rehab center on the ship where he used to conduct sessions. They had been there once, so it was not difficult to find. Ramesh had hired several staffs. The center was renamed as "Digital Nirvana". Ramesh greeted Satvik and Sandeep at the center.

"Your center has grown manifold in last six months, now it is looking like a professional corporate training center," said Satvik.

"It is a different kind of setup than the clinic that I was running in Mumbai. Patients who visited me in Mumbai clinic were all physically ill. It was somewhat easier to diagnose the illness as they had some physical symptoms. Those patients thanked me when they recovered. This center is completely different. Here you will find everyone looks perfectly healthy. They have no physical problems, but all of them are anxious and depressed. They realize that technology has snatched their lives away and they need to reclaim that. All of these people visit this place for a specific reason – anxiety due to social media addiction."

For the first time, Satvik and Sandeep had the opportunity to see the other side of Paybook – user's perspective, and it was not very encouraging. Paybook was not only bad for its founders but was affecting its users severely as well.

"Ramesh, looking at the number of people here, I guess this center might be quite popular and you must be having a phenomenal business," asked Satvik.

"Thanks to the social media frenzy, there are more people today reaching the breaking point and they are seeking help. More people want to reclaim their lives from digital captivity. My teaching and practice here provide them with some glimmer of hope. You would not believe, but it has only spread due to word of mouth," replied Ramesh.

"But I still see more and more people getting addicted to social media, it is not coming down. I am surprised to know that people have started to realize this as a menace now and seeking help," asked Sandeep.

"Well, not everyone is aware of the malaise. I know because I lost my family due to this. Few wise people surely realize that they need to extricate themselves from this technology trap – it is a call to 'digital minimalism' because our lives have been hacked. Our happiness and appreciation of the usual things in life are disappearing fast. We are all becoming more worried and depressed with ourselves. Since this is a new problem, no one really knows how to solve this. Even I am learning about the nature of this problem bit by bit," replied Ramesh.

"And what has been your key learnings so far. What do people do at this center?" asked Satvik.

"My approach is different. I don't go about teaching the ill effects of social media – that does not help. My approach is rather inward-looking and soul searching. In this digital age, I teach them just to be aware of how their mind is driving them crazy. If they can control their own mind, they can very well control the world around them, including their addiction to distractions like social media. Some people call it mindfulness, but you can give it different names like meditation, yoga or spirituality. Let me explain this in detail: -

Today few people are suffering from physical illnesses. At least we have a cure for many diseases, medical science has made enough progress on the front. The healthy body, however, does not guarantee a happy and purposeful life. Our mind poses new sets of problems – it is so volatile. Most minds are surely impacted by the incessant craving for novel activities and suffer from the boredom. We get stressed by the fear of boredom and our mind tries to find something exciting all the time. This is a perpetual problem because the mind quickly discards the fleeting pleasure resulting from an activity in search of something new. Now if we allow the mind to take control of ourselves, we will be lost in this never-ending chase. This is what is happening with most of the digital age people today. Let me explain this with respect to anxiety resulting from social media.

We always share the most exciting things in our lives that we do, be it an exotic vacation that we enjoyed, a marathon that we ran or some medal that we won. Our Facebook timelines usually consist of such posts that depict how our lives have been full of events and activities. We count these as our achievements that eventually make us happy, or at least we think so. We all complain but secretly long for a busy life because that's when we feel our relevance in our setup. One of my friends told me once that the reason he is more worried about the old age is precisely that – irrelevance and dull life.

A dull life that lacks events and activities is no one's envy. I am yet to see a Facebook post that proudly shares – 'today, I did nothing'. Even if there was one – no one would have ever liked it. We fear being idle, our mind finds it scary.

Our cellphones are the best friends to kill the boredom. Even while we wait for less than five minutes on a bus stand, we find it very boring to do nothing. We catch up with social media during that time. It is not just that, often we multi-task. We plan to do multiple things simultaneously to avoid boredom. If you attend a conference or visit a concert today, you can easily find half of the audience engrossed with their cellphones. Our mind needs more and more activity and races all the time. Our mind has got addicted to meaningless activities that are nothing but distractions. We have all become distraction chasers. Social media adds fuel to this addiction. When on Facebook, we see everyone's life is so eventful, we feel sad and anxious that we have been left out.

If we think that this maddening race of activity is what our makes our mind happy, the evolution psychology teaches us otherwise.

Let us go back to 20 years, there was no internet and no cellphone. The letter was the predominant means to communicate. The postal mail took many weeks to reach the destination, and any response was at least a month away. Today we shoot an email, and next moment we get a reply from the other corner of the world. If we don't get a response within a few minutes, we become anxious. Maybe 20 years later we can also expect a similar reply from someone on Mars. With such a lightning pace of development, we should have been several times happier than our forefathers.

The mind does not care about the absolute speed of events or activities, it only senses the relative speed, relative to the previous activity it was engaged in or what it perceives externally. We can feel stationary in a flight even at 1000 km per hour, our mind recognizes the activity of the things only in our proximity. The more active we become, the more our brain craves for further activities to get a similar kick. The brain only knows the acceleration, not the uniform speed. That is why today people with more active lives are more prone to boredom and depression.

The best way to kill boredom is to slow down completely and do something quite boring and stick to it till the time the brain starts absorbing it. The most boring thing for the mind is doing nothing. Though it may sound easy, doing nothing is the most challenging task because our brains are wired for activities.

Another name of doing nothing is 'mindfulness' when you force the maddening craving for an activity to come to screeching halt, the mind's zero error is reset, and it can start perceiving the activity in the small events around us.

So, at this center, I really teach people how to embrace boredom in their life and enjoy it. Some people call is a boring center of happiness. This is what we practice at this wellness center – mindfulness. The basic idea of mindfulness is to be aware and accept the vagaries of your own mind even if you are not able to control it completely."

"I never imagined people will get paid to teach how to get bored, but I must say in this digital age your argument could be compelling. No wonder your center is getting so popular. At this rate, all the social media will shut down eventually, and no one will ever even use our Paybook," Satvik said.

"I don't think so, take an example of other addictions - many people know that cigarette and alcohol are bad for health. There is scientific research to prove that conclusively. There are numerous rehab centers that teach this day-in and day out. Still, most addicts do not pay any attention to it. That's how addiction works, you may have all the knowledge of the ill effects, but some part of your mind forces you to ignore it somehow," said Ramesh.

"I think people will get eventually exhausted with social media. These fads have a limited life cycle. We thought we would make money till the time it lasts," Satvik said.

"Exactly, last time when we met you, our Paybook was riding on this wave. We were very bullish about our prospect. We thought you were too naïve trying to tide against the current. Just in one year, it seems like a reversal of fortune. When we started this business, we thought Paybook was the most futuristic business, after all, social media has been growing like anything. Now talking to you, it seems social media rehab centers are better business than ours," Sandeep agreed.

"Many social researchers are predicting that with the rise of automated technology and wealth, humans will be confronted with a unique problem – what to do with the free time they get. They need to be engaged somehow, else the society will explode. That's why social media is not going to disappear anytime soon, rather it may get morphed into something like virtual reality," replied Ramesh.

"This is what we thought when we started our Paybook. We thought we had created a perfect time pass for our future generations. We were right in our observation but could not think of all these problems we have landed into today," said Sandeep.

"I am surprised to hear that, I believed Paybook was doing great business. Though I think it negatively impacts the society, I understood that the app was very popular with the users," asked Ramesh.

Satvik told Ramesh the entire story, how they were losing money on a daily basis, users were getting more demanding, the IT minister wanted control of the platform, and the police wanted unfettered surveillance. One of his partner Ashok had been indicted on charges for being complicit in illegal activities in Paybook. They seemed to have created a Frankenstein monster.

"We are in a terrible situation Ramesh, and we were wondering if you could help us. We are in a similar situation when you left Mumbai and came to Goa to start this new life. We have been devastated by our social media misadventure."

"I am sure the situation did not turn that bad overnight. Why didn't you sell off the business or shut it down, at least you could have cut your losses?" asked Ramesh.

"We tried selling but could not find buyers. Shutting down would have been akin to running the risk of riots. We unintentionally raised expectations. Now the users believe that we owe them the money for their time on Paybook, for some of them it has become an employment. If we shut down Paybook, they will come after our lives. We will end up in jail for one or the other charges of cheating. Imagine a bar owner who invites customers by paying them to get drunk. After some time, the same customers become a liability – we have become like that," Sandeep replied.

"You have a large user group, but instead of becoming an asset, it has become a liability for you. To get rid of your platform, you must get rid of your users. However, I see a silver lining in the same – you have a database of most addicted social media users. This is an important source of target group who can subscribe to my program. If we can attract those addicted users to our center on mindfulness, I am sure we can also generate good money from it," Ramesh gave a novel business idea.

"How can we do that?"

"There are easy ways, recall the scary pictures they put on the cigarette pack. We can do something similar."

"How are you so confident that you would be able to convince the Paybook addicts to come out of it?"

"Based on my experience of the last year I can tell you, they will not only enjoy this experience but also pay for it. It will be helpful to them as well."

"But the biggest problem is to make them understand how bad it has been for their own well-being. To implement this, we will have to adopt some radical approach," Sandeep said.

"There is a way to tackle the overactive user if they are really causing your financial loss. I would rather explain that by my personal experience.

"During our college days, our professors really wanted to encourage class participation as he thought that was the best mechanism to learn. To facilitate the same, he started awarding some marks for asking a question, providing comments, endorsing views etc. This had a very positive impact on the class environment and most of the people who wanted a good score in the paper started contributing. This however created a different kind of problem. Some over-enthusiastic students would never stop asking questions and providing comments. This started affecting the learning environment in a negative way. The professor thought hard to come up with a solution – finally, he introduced the concept of negative class participation. If someone tried to monopolize the discussion, he was penalized with negative points. This made the overzealous students not to hijack the objective," explained Ramesh.

"This is insightful, possibly we can think of negative Paybook points to manage our hyperactive users."

"How do you run your wellness program? I have attended some digital detox and *vipasana* kind of things that help people calm down and discover themselves spiritually. This is typically conducted in serene natural setup, away from the hustle and bustle of the city lives," asked Satvik.

"I think the best way to understand would be to experience it yourself. Even though you may not be a social media addict, but I am sure your usage would be on the higher side. You can benefit from this program," replied Ramesh.

Satvik thought it was a good idea, but suddenly he remembered the mobile throwing challenge as an entry test for the program. After some persuasion from Sandeep, he agreed to take the plunge.

Knowing Our Problems

The first day was more of a classroom session but still, something was unique in the spacious set up on deck. Satvik had been to the casino ship last time, but this felt completely opposite. There was very little noise other than the sound of the waves gently hitting the bottom of the ship. It was like the same cruise from the outside but entirely different inside.

Satvik thought it resembled the religious ashram more than the corporate training centers. Everyone was sitting on the floor in a Yoga posture. There was a giant Buddha statue by Ramesh's side. The ambience inside was calm and serene.

There were 15 more participants attending the session, all sitting in five rows of three each. They all appeared of different ages - 6 of them looked like middle-aged women, 2 teenaged girls and 7 men in late 40s. After the initial pleasantries and brief introduction, Ramesh started the session.

"The first objective of our program is for every one of us to assess our relationship with social media objectively and why we think there is a need to reset that relationship. Sometimes it may be embarrassing to admit how much we are dependent on our cell phones every waking moment, but the acknowledgement of the problem is the first step towards the solution. In one of my previous batch, I asked everyone to take a two-minute break every hour and write down on a paper amount of time that they spent on their phone in the last hour. To their own surprise, they found out that it was almost one third during a busy workday and three fourth during a relaxed holiday. This is a very simple exercise that we all can do."

"When do we say that the phone usage has become an addiction, what is the breaking point?" asked one of the teenaged girls.

"It is a straightforward test, I will ask three questions if the answer to all of them is yes then you can conclude that you have reached the breaking point: -

"Do you check your social media as the first thing when you wake up in the morning?

"Do you check your social media feeds as the last thing before you sleep?"

"Do you carry your phone to the washroom at home?"

The girl nodded yes, all the three times, but so did everyone else in the room.

"Last week, my infant son, who is just 15 months, was playing with a magazine in the house. He started crying after some time. When I closely observed, he was trying to double-tap to enlarge a toy picture in the magazine," a lady spoke.

Everyone burst into laughter.

"It is becoming a real problem even for adults like us. For a long time, people believed that addiction can only be explained from a biological perspective like drugs, alcohol or other substances. However, many researchers today believe that there is another form of addiction called behavioral addiction and social media is a fitting example for the same," replied Ramesh.

"But addiction as a problem is not new to society, something or the other has always been there," commented Satvik.

"True, addiction has been there always, possibly it has some evolutionary explanations as well. For example, many of us today are compulsive sweet eaters. It had evolved in our genes through thousands of years when our forefathers were hunters and gatherers. Whenever the forager encountered some sweet fruits or honey, the only option was to eat as much as possible before moving on from that location. There was no possibility to store anything those days. Even today, this behavior is reflected when we see the food of our liking, even though we have very advanced storage abilities. This behavior is so ingrained in our genes that today overeating is a bigger cause of worry than hunger. The idea of this session is that we scrutinize our own behavior from a more rational perspective.

"The learning methodology here is an honest discussion about yourself. I would encourage all of you to share your personal perspectives," said Ramesh.

"My name is Rajesh and I am working at middle managerial level in an IT company. I always feel an urge to check my Facebook and when I start, I can't stop my fingers from scrolling further and further. There is always something new there and I fear that I might miss out on something. To avoid this fear, I always feel like catching up with Facebook updates. I am never really content with the same, it goes on in a loop."

"Rajesh, that is the first sign of worry. In psychological parlance, it is called **FOMO** (Fear of missing out). This term is increasingly being used to explain the anxiety people have when they fear they might miss out on experiences, events or social conversations that might be happening at any moment. When one keeps scrolling through the Facebook status updates for hours, the underlying psychology is the same. The fear of being left out triggers excessive smartphone use and is eventually responsible for creating more insecurities and stress in the users."

"Yes, and it is never-ending because the Facebook feeds never stop, the more I scroll, the more I feel the need to do the same. I had a similar issue with internet browsing and news reading earlier, but this problem is even more severe," replied Rajesh.

"The comparison with internet browsing addiction is interesting. When you are browsing through the internet content, the topics are still somewhat related, and it is a linear engagement for the brain. Social media posts, on the contrary, are very diverse – discussions jump from one topic to another one randomly. This may appear stimulating but is quite stressful for the mind. The other important difference is Facebook is a two-way feed, we get interested in the comments shared by our friends more than the posts themselves. Since these are the people in our peer group, we seriously value their comments and mentally engage with the same," Ramesh explained.

"I usually don't comment on the posts. In fact, I am not an active user, I don't even post quite often. Still, I feel the urge to scroll through Facebook pages and I feel awful at the end of the day," another man who was listening to the conversation very intently, commented.

"That is called passive browsing and it has been accepted even by Facebook that it could be more problematic. As per a research, people who do not engage actively with the contents but silently browse through them are more at the risk of feeling inadequate and anxious. In one experiment, University of Michigan students randomly assigned to just go through Facebook for 10 minutes were in a worse mood *at the end of the day than students assigned to post or talk to friends on Facebook,"* replied Ramesh.

"That is surprising, some mediums like TV news or even newspaper we always consume passively but that was never a problem," replied Satvik.

149

"Yes, that is because TV, newspaper or book do not talk back or evoke comparison. Unlike Facebook, we do not have a conversation with them. All of us believe we occupy a fixed place in the social hierarchy. Some information we discard because it does not belong to our group, for example as a middle class we may not relate to the contents related to very poor or very rich even if we may empathize with them. The real comparison comes when posts happen to be from our peer group. In social media, we generally have people like us, so we have a greater tendency to engage," replied Ramesh.

"Another reason that passive users feel anxiety is that the social media posts are highly curated bordering on perfection – a perfect family photo, a perfect holiday video creates more dichotomy between the real life and the projected life. The farther we get from reality, the more stress we invite when we hit routine humdrum of our daily lives.

"Another sign of addiction I have seen is that people start using their phone even in a face to face conversation. I almost feel insulted at those instances though I may be guilty of doing the same at times," said Satvik.

"In social media parlance, it is called phubbing. Phubbing as per the Oxford dictionary is the practice of ignoring one's companion or companions in order to pay attention to one's phone or other mobile devices. This term was coined as a blend of phone and snubbing. It is defined as behavior where the smartphone user starts focusing on the phone in the course of normal face to face conversation. It is not very uncommon to see people using their phones while in an informal meeting or social setup. The person who gets ignored is called phubee and the one with phone addiction is called phubber.

"The psychologists have written extensive papers on this behavior and how it undermines the social interaction as the problematic behavior gets slowly normalized and phubee starts becoming phubber. In large conferences and concerts, you would hear the announcements at the beginning to put phones on silent mode, but at any point, you can be sure that half of the audience would be fiddling with their smartphones."

"I think women are more addicted to social media than men. Are there any research findings?" One of the women in the group asked.

"Since social media is so new, there is hardly any exhaustive research available on these topics. However, some sporadic researches have shown that women are more extensive users of smartphones than men. While men still somewhat use the smartphone for traditional communication like talking, women are more inclined to use it primarily to keep in touch with friends through social media. Picture sharing sites are usually more popular with women. Platforms like Instagram and Pinterest are more popular among woman. As per Pew research, 73% of women use social media in the US compared to 65% of men. The percentage of usage by women has been consistently higher over the last 10 years. A recent study of more than 23,500 participants between the age group of 16 and 88 found that single women are the most likely to be addicted to social media," Ramesh responded.

"I get a very irresistible urge to check my social media feed even during odd hours like driving. I just find it very difficult to wait at the signals. I start fiddling with my phone by the time the traffic lights turn red," another young man asked.

"You are not alone, 90% of the drivers in the US admit to using smartphone while driving, 50% among them do so to check their social media updates. AT&T in the US recently launched a campaign "it can wait" where it is urging the drivers to take a pledge that they would not use cell phones while driving. On an average, 9 people are killed daily and more than 1000 injured in the US due to smartphone distraction while driving."

"But what if we use hands-free?"

"Hand usage of a phone is bad but even the hands-free are not any better. Talking to someone remotely on the phone while driving could be equally accident-prone," replied Ramesh.

"Can the same argument not be applied when we talk to our fellow passengers in the car?"

"When you are talking to a fellow passenger in the car, he or she has an equal stake in the safety of the drive. The fellow passenger is equally vigilant and talks only when the road conditions are fine. In contrast, while talking on the phone, the other person has no idea about the road conditions and no stake in the safety," replied Ramesh.

Ramesh explained further, "This constant urge to check your phone gives rise to what is called attention deficit – where one can't focus on the activity at hand. Some psychologists call this 'distraction addiction' that impacts our cognitive function. The complex activity or creative thoughts require a sustained period of peak concentration. So, if one is a writer, scientist, doctor or a sportsperson – the social media addiction can be devastating.

"Attention is an emerging field of study in neuroscience. Human brains have several parts responsible for different functions of human bodies. These parts constantly interact with each other and compete for brain processing resources. The brain chatter can be compared to a noisy restaurant.

"There are lower order brain functions like breathing, blood circulation that happen automatically. However, there is a part of the human brain called frontal cortex right above our eyes that makes us real intelligent creatures. Of all the living beings, humans have the largest size of frontal cortex and scientists believe that this is the basis of cognitive revolution that humans have gone through. This part of the brain performs an executive function that decides where the brain resources should be allocated.

"Of all the living creatures, only humans can voluntarily direct their thoughts irrespective of the sensory inputs they might be getting. This means that you can be sitting in a busy market but can voluntarily cut yourself off from all the distractions and concentrate on some unique thought. The power of concentration is unique to us.

"So, without this frontal cortex, we would all be like animals, living being without very little cognition.

"And during the panic stage or heightened anxiety, this part of the brain gets subdued. That is why when we are angry or depressed, we are more likely to do unreasonable and stupid things which otherwise we would never do.

"This part of the brain also loses its effectiveness when we try to do multi-tasking. Imagine a person walking in the street, listening to a song through his earphones and texting at the same time. There are different brain areas associated with walking, visual sensors, auditory inputs and hand controls. The frontal cortex plays the role of a switching agent that allocates the brain resources in a round robin fashion. But each switching has a cost and time lag that is why you may have seen several funny videos of people bumping onto the lamp posts while texting. Plus, such multi-tasking reduces your memory level. The mobile phones today have added several new dimensions of multi-tasking."

"I recall during the job interviews earlier one of the questions used to be – can you do multitasking? It was considered a great quality," said Satvik.

"That is a big misconception that we all have. Even in the work-life, a manager is expected to attend too many things in parallel. This essentially divides the intensity of attention and eventually, the quality of output. The value of the cognitive output depends on two factor – the length of the uninterrupted time and the intensity of attention. All the renowned innovators are known to have mastered these two skills. Cal Newport, in his book, calls it *deep work*. He gives an example of how psychologist Carl Jung used to retire into a cave-like structure for a long period of time to come up with a philosophy that could challenge someone like Sigmund Freud. Even today some eminent professors at Ivy League universities leading the advanced research, are unapproachable via electronic media."

"When one switches tasks in quick succession, the brain has to deal with what is called *attention residue* –leftover attention of the previous work that eats into the intensity of the current work," explained Ramesh.

"Going by that logic Facebook and Twitter could be a great culprit that can make deep work more difficult," said Sandeep.

"Today, there are 3.1 billion users on Facebook worldwide. The average person spends 2 hours a day, so in total, he or she may be spending more than 5 years of the lifetime only scrolling through the Facebook pages. For teenagers, this could be as high as 9 hours per day. The problem has already reached an epidemic proportion and many people are urging to act in this regard. Some estimates posit that there are 210 million people worldwide who might be suffering from internet and social media addiction," Ramesh added to the astonishment of the audience.

"This is really alarming," Satvik said.

"I suspected that the social media menace was growing but did not realize that it has already reached a clinical level like this. We are all becoming social media prisoners.

"Some people do realize the danger and they are quitting social media like Facebook. Many in the western world are either de-activating or deleting their Facebook account. I have seen many people announcing on their FB page that they are taking a sabbatical but many of them return within no time," stated Satvik.

"Quitting Facebook entirely or any social media is a wrong approach. It is like stopping to drive because motor cars are more unsafe than horse-driven carts. It is like running away from a social setup because it has some problems. Any medium is not good or bad by itself, but it is our inability to understand the right way to use it. I never advise anyone to quit Facebook but be aware of its merits and demerits," explained Ramesh.

"This was precisely the objective of my day 1 session, for all of us to realize the extent to which we are already a digital captive and how it is affecting our own lives and happiness. At the same time, we must understand that it is like spilt milk, it is a technology that can't be undone, and we can't go back to the pre-social media era. We have to learn to live with this beast without becoming a slave to it," Ramesh summed up the conversation.

"I still fail to understand one thing. If we are so upset with social media, we can go ahead and stop using it. Even I have deleted the app whenever I felt I was unnecessarily getting disturbed by it. There are newer apps that help restrict your usage of social media. It can block select apps or restrict usage time. One such app is called Freedom app. There are also other apps that the parents can use to check the usage of the same by their kids," Satvik asked Ramesh.

"Yes, we always have an option to block these apps rather than complaining about it. However, very few people use the Freedom app today. The reason is that social media does serve some purpose, it is not all bad. There are people who feel connected to this world through their virtual identity. There is research available that concludes that people are increasingly trusting the virtual profile more than the real profile. The online marriages last longer as per some statistics," replied Ramesh.

"We should not always condemn Facebook. After all, we also learn so many things from it. There are a lot of news items, motivational posts and even positive bites. It keeps us up to date," remarked Satvik.

"Twenty years back, we needed more and more information to make better decisions, whether about life or business. Access to information was a key success.

"Today, the situation has reversed. The success depends on how successfully one can filter the unnecessary information. Today if you want to research on any topic, you need to weed out the unwanted things. The pattern of learning has changed from being receptive to all knowledge to filtering bulk of the available information – essentially means focusing on the right information," Ramesh countered Satvik.

"This is really unique oversight," Satvik said.

"I have made a simple rule for myself to overcome the information overload. Before reading every article or post, I ask myself if I can really act on that in any way. If not than the news is irrelevant, and I just ignore that," Sandeep was still in control of things.

"The social media has given the power to ordinary people to reach out to any number of audiences at virtually zero cost. It has made stars out of common people like us. It serves a need to connect with people. Earlier the only way to communicate publicly was through a medium like TV, newspaper or Radio, which was restricted to the powerful elites. Social media is empowering in that sense. The problem starts because we don't know how to use it and are never taught about the usage. There is no user manual associated with a Facebook app. It does not even mention what the most optimum way to use it is. It just leaves it to the users to explore it by themselves. Imagine someone buying a car but not knowing how to drive it. Social media has become like that car today. Most of us use it in the wrong way. The key is to learn to use it correctly, but before attempting to do so, we need to understand the way our brain works," Ramesh explained in detail.

"While we are all focusing on Facebook, there is another social media evil – twitter, and it engages people very differently. I fail to understand why there is so much of rage on twitter?" another person asked Ramesh.

"Twitter provides a new and direct way of arguing with strangers on any topic. In real life, we don't start a fierce argument in public places with unknown people. We are very wary of our image and social standing. Twitter, on the other hand, is largely anonymous. Anonymity does strange things to human psychology, it makes an introvert who hardly speaks in public, a fiercely outspoken person," Ramesh replied.

"I know many of my friends who are in competition with each other on the number of twitter followers. I myself have been trying to increase that, but unlike Facebook, you can't send a friend request on twitter. So, it entirely depends on the other persons whether they want to follow you," Satvik said.

"You can always buy followers on twitter as well, there are various packages available," Sandeep replied sarcastically.

"Many of them are bot followers that are created to sell followership. After a few weeks, the followers count drops. However, there are re-fill packages. This has started a new business opportunity for many people who do not know how twitter following works," replied Satvik.

"Just as making people famous, twitter has also been instrumental in harming people. One tweet, if it goes viral, can bring down the reputation of anyone in a few hours.

"Let me tell you about an incident of Justin Sacco in 2013, when she was on a long journey from New York to South Africa. Before she boarded, she tweeted

> *"Going to Africa. Hope I don't get AIDS. Just kidding. I'm white!"*

Of course, it was a tweet in bad taste. There were many people offended. But she had no idea that by the time she landed in South Africa, she would be a worldwide trend.

She had only 170 followers at the time of her tweet. On knowing the enormity of the problem, the PR executive of IAC, where she worked, issued an apology

> *Words cannot express how sorry I am and how necessary it is for me to apologize to the people of South Africa.*

However, the 11-hour gap was far too much. People were so outraged that they targeted her employer and asked them to fire her before she landed. Her employer IAC fired her eventually. Just one casual tweet destroyed her entire career in a moment.

Twitter has given voice to anyone who can type. But there is also a lot of idle entertainment in that. Almost everyone takes a position and expresses himself or herself fiercely. The collective outrage could even eventually destroy our right of free speech because we are all afraid of public shaming," replied Ramesh

"If Facebook has made us envious, twitter has made us angry warriors, we relish in shaming people. In his book *"So, you've publicly been shamed"*, a British Journalist, Jon Ronson describes how twitter has started the practice of public shaming that used to happen in mediaeval Europe. People used to assemble at the town square and publicly shame the subject in question. The practice was discontinued, not due to increasing population and decreasing number of town squares but due to greater call of compassion. The public shaming was too harsh a punishment. Twitter has restarted that at a much larger scale. Jon Ronson interviews many people who have been subjected to such shaming and the devastation that followed in their lives. The worrying thing is that it is even more difficult to control such Twitter shaming these days," responded Sandeep.

"A more fundamental question is how these social media apps are changing our brain for the worse?" said Ramesh.

"Yuval Harari, in his famous book 'Sapiens' talks about the evolution of human brains thousands of years ago. The reasons our brains are bigger in size compared to other animals is because 'we love to gossip'. The excessive inquisitiveness in the lives of other fellow human beings was quite unique to homo sapiens. Since the hunter-gather days, 'the gossip' has always consumed most of our brainpower, more than worrying for food in the jungle or protecting ourselves from animals," Sandeep explained.

"Most of us would feel insulted today that we use our brain mostly for the unproductive task of gossiping and worrying about others," replied Satvik.

"Apes don't worry so much about what the other apes are thinking about them. The maximum they worry about is the natural danger and other animals. Humans, on the other hand, spend most of the time thinking about what fellow human beings are thinking. "

It was an interesting free-flowing discussion that Ramesh was facilitating. In the end, he announced, "This pretty much fulfills the objective of day 1, we wanted to probe our relationship with social media in a free-wheeling discussion to understand this problem and the extent of damage it is causing to all of us."

Adapting Ourselves

"Do you know the biggest reason for our stress today?" Ramesh asked the people in the audience who had diligently assembled early morning at six am the next day.

"Challenging work," replied one.

"Modern lifestyle and travel," replied another.

A person in the early fifties described it in more detail - "I would say the biggest reason is – technology enslavement, and most of us are aware of it. The strange thing is though I know that it causes anxiety, whenever I tried to fix that, I had withdrawal syndrome. Let me tell you my story to explain this better.

"Last year I went on a cruise holiday with my wife, something that we had been planning for many years. I thought this would be a good experiment in digital absenteeism. Initially, it seemed like a wonderful escape from the daily humdrum at work, but soon this all changed. My mind was still pre-occupied with the developments at my office. I had submitted a project proposal before I left the office for the vacation. Though my manager had approved, few colleagues had raised questions. This project was significant for my promotion.

"I felt a strong urge to check my emails. To my agony, there was no internet on the cruise. Now suddenly I was cut off from my active world. The more I tried to avoid that thought of being disconnected, it came back to haunt. My wife was happy about it, but I started feeling severe anxiety. It increased slowly, and soon it spread to different parts of my body and I started feeling pain. By the end of the third day, my condition was so bad that the moment our cruise returned, I had to be rushed to the hospital. The doctor confirmed after the check-up that I had a heart attack. I am sure this was triggered by the anxiety of being cut-off from the network. This time I realized that the email addiction had become so problematic."

"Some of these addictions work like the boiling frog example. When you put a frog in water and slowly start heating the water, the frog does not make any attempt to jump out. Only when the water becomes too hot, it realizes the danger and tries to come out of it. By that time, its muscles become too weak to jump out of the boiling pot. It eventually dies. Some of these technological addictions today work like that. The stress keeps increasing till the time it overpowers us, it causes anxiety if we don't attend to it," explained Ramesh.

A young girl in the audience commented, "During our exam times in the college some of us found it very difficult to stay away from Facebook despite knowing that we might fail in the exam if we did not study. Especially with WhatsApp, we could not stop ourselves. In fact, social media activities increased during such time.

"Some of us found a way around it finally. We used to give our passwords to our friends who would change it during the exam days and would lock us out of the social media. A crude way but this shows the helplessness we experienced," she explained further.

"The multiple gadgets that we have today has helped us shrink the constraint of time and space. Our past, present and future have all got mixed up, and we live in a multi-dimensional world. Earlier, our stress was limited as we experienced only the immediate environment. Now there is no constraint of distance. So, we might get worried about an incident that might happen thousands of miles away in distant future," Satvik seemed to agree with Ramesh on this.

"The most important reason that we face stress today is because we don't live in the present moment. More than 90% of the time, our mind is either living in the past or worrying about the future. We don't live here and now. Our body always lives in the present, but our mind cleverly escapes our body to wander into all kind of negative thoughts. It always appears as our mind is flying at high speed and our body is trying to catch up with the same. There is a dichotomy of the mind and body that creates stress in all of us.

Thousands of years back when our forefathers were hunter and gatherers, they always lived in the moment. Incidentally, they had very little to plan for. When they felt hungry, they went for hunting. There was nothing to store for the future. They had very little control over their external environment. The animals could outrun them, or some other dangerous animals could hunt them too. Life was so unpredictable that there was little sense worrying about the same. They moved from one place to another place and mostly were at the mercy of nature for their survival. They lived one moment to another moment.

With adoption of agriculture, the human settlement started. They domesticated animals for their own use. They also realized that there were so many things the humans could plan like how much food to grow. They planned their work for different seasons. They no longer wanted food for the day but for weeks, months and even years in advance. With excess food supply, they created granaries and protected them from animals and thieves. At this time in human evolution, brain spent more time in future worries than living in the present moment."

"That is a very fascinating perspective. Does it mean our hunter and gatherer forefathers were happier than the more sophisticated agriculturists?" asked Satvik.

"That's what many historians believe. Even though the average life span of humans has increased, they were not necessarily a happier lot. The same can be extrapolated to the modern age with internet and social media. Today our brain is trained not only to incessantly think about the future but also the past. This pattern of skipping the current moment has got so ingrained in us that we have forgotten how to live 'here and now' and it has made us a miserable lot," Said Ramesh.

"We will do a small exercise today to return to our original state of mindfulness," Ramesh took up the role of an instructor from a teacher in evolutionary history.

"All of you sit comfortably, cross your legs and be in a fully relaxed posture. Take out your spectacles and keep them by the side. Any tight or straining object on your body like a watch, you can remove. Let the body be in perfectly no strain state.

"Now clasp your hands together and close your eyes."

Slowly the audience transported themselves into the meditative state, there was complete silence for some time.

"Concentrate on your breath as you inhale and exhale. Focus on the tip of your nose, you will get the sensation of inhaling cold air and exhaling hot air from your lungs.

"Let the thoughts wander, don't try to control the same. But when your thoughts wander, observe it passively how your mind is jumping from one thought to another thought, just like a monkey that keeps jumping from one branch to another branch. The focus will slowly come back to breathing and the tip of the nose. Just keep in mind that thoughts are not you. You are not your body but a third party that dispassionately observes the body, the mind and the interplay of the two.

"It may sound ironical, but most of us do not know how to breathe so that it rejuvenates our entire body. Take a deep breath and exhale slowly – focus on how the cool air enters through your nose, passes through the lungs and provides energy to the whole body for the moment.

"Now we are in the last two minutes of this session. Continue the focus on your breath. Let the mind wander but bring it back and slowly focus on different parts of your body - one organ at a time, starting from the top of your head slowly to your shoulder, arms, hip and finally to the tip of your toes. This is called 'mindfulness' – you are focusing on your present breath and parts of your body.

"In neurobiology, we teach that the brain has the entire map of the body. The neurons in our brain are connected to almost all the body organs. The brain controls the functioning of these organs; that is why we can breathe, walk and talk. Many of these controls are automated, like blood pressure, digestion, breathing. They work in the subconscious domain. Many other controls, like voluntary movements, operate in the conscious mind. All our organs have a projection in the brain. In other words, our brain has a body map. For a long time even in medical science, it was taught as if a small man with a visual representation of our body lived in our brain. This man also had a name – 'homunculus'. Try to experience that man in your mind – that is mindfulness.

"The purpose of meditation is to concentrate on the projection of the brain and scan through your entire body

165

by just scanning through the mind. This increases the mind-body co-ordination that can help to lead a healthy mind.

"Friends, we are in the last 30 seconds of the session, I will reverse count 5 and at the end of the same slowly rub your palms and put them on your eyes and gently open when you are ready.

"We have completed just 10 minutes of quick mindfulness exercise. How do you feel at the end of this?" asked Ramesh.

"It was relaxing," replied one person.

"I felt pain in some part of the body," said another one.

"It was really good but to tell you honestly, I dozed off," replied Satvik.

"Maybe that's what your body truly needed. Most of the time, we ignore the cry from our body. We are too pre-occupied by our mind. Bringing the mind to a halt brings us more in consonance with the body. When our body and mind are in synch, we are most likely to experience happiness and contentment. In our daily lifestyle, mostly our physical body is stationary, but the mind is racing at high speed. We need to increase the physical activity of the body and reduce the speed of thoughts in our mind."

"Is there any scientific basis of mindfulness. I have heard that it is primarily a religious act?" asked a lady in the audience.

"Some do think that it has a religious angle given its origin in yoga and Hinduism. However, there has been extensive research on mindfulness in recent years in all western universities. Today it is pretty much considered a mainstream field of scientific study in Harvard, MIT etc. I recently read an article that mindfulness is being introduced as a subject for school students in New York City."

"But how do you control the worry of the future. If you fear something terrible is going to happen, how you can avoid thinking about it?" asked one person.

Ramesh told a small story.

> There was a king who went to a sage to ask about his future events and outcomes.
>
> "Why do you want to know about your future outcomes?" asked the sage.
>
> "So that if something bad is going to happen, I can change it."
>
> "If you can change the thing that is going to happen, it will never happen, so it will not be your future in that sense."
>
> The king realized the folly of his argument, but this time he flipped it.
>
> "I want to know my future so that if something good is going to happen, I feel happy about it," said the king.
>
> "If something good is going to happen to you in future, knowing it now would deprive you of the happiness that you would have got were you not expecting it in advance."
>
> The King got the idea. The knowledge of future outcome was practically of no value to him, so worrying about the future was meaningless.

"That is a nice perspective, but don't we need to plan, set goals and work towards that? If we completely ignore the future, we will be acting blind," asked Satvik.

"There is a difference between planning, acting and worrying about the outcomes. Most of us invariably indulge in the latter.

"The biggest worry is worrying about the concerns of the future.

"Our minds are trained to consider the worst outcome as the most probable outcome, even if it is far less likely. We assign undue weightage to the unfavorable outcome and prepare ourselves for the worst. Again, this is an evolutionary thing and it was very much required when our ancestors faced a lot of external dangers. For example, even if there was the faintest probability of an animal possibly hiding in the bush could be a lion, our mind pressed the panic button and we started running at the top speed. More often, it could well be an illusion, just like we think of a small rope as a snake in the dark.

"During pre-historic days, this was fine from a survival point of view. In our brains, there is a unique organ called 'amygdala' that orchestrates such fight or flight response and channelizes entire bodily resources to counter the perceived threat. But today, the dangers in our daily lives have reduced. We need not have that fatalist view and assign excessive weightage to the worst outcome. That way, we can keep a sense of realism intact," responded Ramesh.

"The same logic applies when we look at past events. I used to feel a lot of anger when I used to think about my past. Why it all had to happen with me only. Then I slowly realized that the events of the past and future have no intrinsic value in the present. Even if you recall a past event that has good memories, the mind craves for it again and thus adds to the stress. So, it does not matter whether the past has been happy or sad but thinking about it, in any case, can make one anxious. Our body does not care for it, just that our mind gets stuck with it," he added further.

"But does the social media addiction adds to this stress. How the 'mindfulness – here and now' can help in overcoming this situation?"

"Thanks to social media, there is little space between the things that are happening around and the things that are happening to self. We have expanded our sense of self. We imagine ourselves pretty much at the center of the world and we presume everyone, and everything must work for having a positive impact on us. We believe that the world exists to keep us happy, it has an obligation to us. So, we build a strong point of view for each event and every person around us. Hence the incident that in a pre-social media would have been completely irrelevant to us, suddenly feels important and our imaginary well-being starts depending on it. We constantly struggle to find our relevance in the physical world, but it manifests in the overindulgence in social media.

"When you browse through the angry tweets, you can understand why people feel so enraged. We have lost our ability to see things without judging them. Everything must be either good or bad. Either we like or dislike, love or hate. It divides us into binaries. Mind is always comfortable dealing with the binaries because then it knows how to react to the same with different emotions that are nothing but preconfigured algorithms of the past.

"What mindfulness does is, it creates a space between our mind and the external world and events. It creates a pause between our stimuli and our reactions. It allows us to appreciate that most things around us just happen, they don't have to happen to us. Many things exist, they don't exist exclusively for us. Our peace of mind will be driven not by how much the world events are beneficial to us but how much we can train our mind to think nonchalantly," Ramesh explained again.

"There is a difference between a 'trained mind' and 'untrained mind'. The world exists exclusively in our mind. In spirituality, it is said that one way to study the world is to study our own self. Mindfulness essentially teaches this; it helps us control the impulse that makes us angry and stressed.

"Internet today keep us connected to the external world every moment, be it work-related, news, social media posts or phone calls. This practically keeps our brain looking for the threatening signal round the clock. This has reduced our attention span and focus. It is like watching many movies simultaneously and trying to make sense of them. Our mind did not have enough time to evolve to deal with this situation of information overload. The challenge today is to filter out irrelevant information and be comfortable with it," Ramesh explained.

"Today, we all are obsessed with our cellphones. Any important event good or bad we see everyone flashes out the cell phone and start recording or taking pictures. Most of the people miss the joy of the moment just to capture it in their camera," someone from the audience asked.

"And the most tragic thing is most of us never go back to see those videos or photos. It is just like we buy many things never to use in the future because buying is so convenient, and we have money," replied Ramesh.

The third day of the program was slightly different from the first two days. All participants were made to sit in front of their computers. They all had to wear a small cap that had some wires protruding like one of those sci-fi characters.

"This is called EEG and it will measure the electromagnetic waves in your brain."

Ramesh asked everyone to consciously focus on the screen. The only condition was that they had to cover at least 100 different social media posts or news items without any break in between for four continuous hours.

At the end of the session, Ramesh asked all the participants how they felt.

"Stressed and tensed," replied one person, "when the topic changed the mind had to quickly adjust to the next context before it felt fully exhausted."

"This can also be verified from the neural activities in your brains that were captured by the EEG graphs," Ramesh gave everyone the copy.

"Sometimes back scientists discovered a special type of neurons in human brains called "mirror neurons". These neurons were accidentally discovered in an experiment with monkeys where the same neurons fired whether the monkey was performing the task (eating in this case) or it was watching others perform that task. This means similar emotional response can get biologically triggered by watching others do something as if we were doing the same act. This is the reason we feel sad when we see others cry or laughter is contagious. This is probably the most important basis of civilization – because we feel empathy for others. This is also the basis of tribes and social groups. Though evolution tells us about the survival of the fittest theory, humans have long discovered that there is a greater value in co-operation. This makes us highly social animal – our sense of well-being does not entirely depend on our individual well-being but the collective well-being of the social group we relate to. We sometimes compete and sometimes collaborate, but the actions of our fellow human being always evoke an emotional response in us.

"A trained brain is not afraid of boredom, it embraces that. So, if you are a scientist, a doctor, an artist or an author, you need to first get used to the boredom and let the mind be content with it. As a neurosurgeon, I can tell you that it is like tuning the reward system of your brain in such a way that it no longer seeks novelty every other moment," Ramesh provided a detailed explanation on the working on human brains.

The second half of the program consisted of four-hour trekking in the jungle of North Goa. It passed through a green forest, several water streams and uninhabited areas. There was no traffic noise. It was a peaceful surrounding away from the hustle and bustle of the city. The hours of walking made all of them tired. Every muscle of their body was paining. Though their body had drained out, the surrounding full of greenery had a calming effect on the mind.

"Nature has the power to refill our energy sources. That is why the monks found solace in the mountains in the earlier time. It rejuvenates our brain cells and naturally de-stresses us. Nature always lives in the present – the trees, rivers, and animals," said Ramesh.

"Now we can understand the contrast in our experience between the first half activities of internet browsing and the second activity of trekking in the jungle. In the first four hours, the mind was exhausted, but the body was resting. In the second half, the body was dead tired, but the mind was still fresh. But overall, I still feel that the second part of the activity was so rejuvenating," replied Satvik.

"Exactly, the idea was to experience that we similarly need a phone life balance in our daily lives to manage stress. Genetically we have evolved to do more of physical activity and less of sedentary activities. The caveman applied their mind, but they ran faster when they went hunting. Incidentally, in modern times, we are expected to perform a lot more cognitive functions than physical activities. While some of us do take care of the body by physical exercise, we almost always neglect our mental well-being. Thanks to advancement in medicine and our longer life expectancy, we are more likely to suffer from mental health issues than physical illness. And many of these can be prevented by little awareness and a better lifestyle," said Ramesh.

This was a pretty impactful session for Sandeep and Satvik. They understood why people were interested in such a program run by Ramesh. At the end of the day, everyone wants to be happy. If happiness can be achieved by reducing the stress in our daily lives, there will be more people signing up for the same. The key thing is that this must be experienced first to believe it. Once the person has experienced it, he or she is quite unlikely to go back to the mindless addiction of technology.

In the evening, Satvik and Sandeep were taking a stroll on the beach again. It had been a long but very insightful day. Two years back walking on this beach, they had come up with the idea of Paybook and their roller coaster ride had begun.

They went to the same restaurant where the three friends had met first fondly talking about the events of the past. This time the restaurant was noisy, full of cacophonous sound. Few young people were dancing nearby.

"I had an awful day today," Shalini called up.

"What happened?" Satvik could barely hear what she was trying to say.

"Ashok came to our house today and he kind of created a scene. He was shouting at the top of his voice that he was fabricated by you and Sandeep. He said he dedicated all his effort and time in nurturing Paybook but got backstabbed by the two of you."

"Ok, what does he want?"

"He wants to take complete control of Paybook and wants you guys to be out of this company. His party has directed him to use it for political advertising."

"But the company is making huge losses, and we don't have any investor to bail us out," Satvik said.

"He said it does not bother him. He was never into this for money. As for the losses, some NGOs have agreed to fund for the time being. He refused to share the details," replied Shalini.

"Really, I thought he would be distraught with all the recent happenings and would want to stay away from all this."

"You are forgetting that he is a politician and he has been through such ordeals even before. For people like him being arrested is not the end of the world. In fact, Ashok has become more aggressive in demanding full control of the company. I told him that you are away in Goa. He said he would come back again tomorrow," replied Shalini.

"Tell him that both I and Sandeep want to move out from Paybook, and he will have complete control over it from now on."

Shalini could not believe what she heard, after all, Paybook was Satvik's brainchild, and Sandeep had used his technical know-how for this.

"But what happens to your investments, your dream of making it the next Facebook of our times? We already have a huge customer base and a data bank than can be used for multiple purposes," asked Shalini.

"We have to find a bigger and better dream, and as long as Paybook is concerned, we are done with it. Our idea has run its course. Now it has only become a weapon that can be used for undesirable purposes. Possibly it has some use for Ashok. For us, it has little intrinsic business value," replied Satvik.

'Though I said that without much thought, it couldn't have been timed any better,' Satvik thought. As an astute businessman, he never took an impulsive decision – especially if it amounted to any financial loss. In this case, he saw it more as an opportunity to cut his losses. Paybook was anything but a good business idea.

The music at the restaurant got louder, another group of college student joined the dance. The dance floor was spotted by multicolored light beams. A surveillance jeep passed nearby flashing the full beam on the pitch-dark sea beach.

Sandeep asked Satvik, "What is the new idea that you were talking about?"

"As Paybook, we successfully hacked people's lives. But soon I realized that we were riding a tiger. For us, Paybook was becoming a loose cannon with every passing day. Just as we realized it, our users will eventually realize it as well. The mindfulness session by Ramesh has provided me with a completely new perspective, I am happy that we met him.

"We will create a new app that will help everyone reclaim their lives from technological enslavement. Technology is not a villain, but it needs to be managed to realize our potential. We will use technology to manage the ill effects of technology. We will use the latest research in brain science not to create another app like Paybook but to manage ourselves in the age of Paybook.

"We will partner with Ramesh and create business offerings on mindfulness practice. Our offering will not only generate profits for us but also make people happier. A business model like that is more profitable and futuristic."

"What will we call it?" asked Sandeep.

"Mindfulness 2.0."

Epilogue – 5 years later

Mindfulness 2.0 is a top-rated course across the age groups. Now it has 200-acre sprawling campus, but it has retained the natural setting and quiet surroundings. At any point, there are at least a thousand participants in various programs. The mindfulness program has become very popular and has spread into multiple centers across India.

The main center in Goa also got a research center on mindfulness. It has become a living experimental setting where people are discovering a balanced use of technology in their lives.

It is not about anti-technology or the digital detox, there are many programs like that available already. It is about establishing a balanced relationship with social media by controlling our own intents and behaviors. There is a digital version of the program as well, and that is becoming more popular every passing day. It was the brainchild of Satvik, and Sandeep had created; an immersive virtual reality game on a similar theme. Mindfulness 2.0 has become a lifestyle app that focuses on mental well-being and controls any obsessive behavior. Some people also call this a 'Happiness App'.

Satvik is so happy to switch to this from Paybook. Apart from the peace of mind, it also turned out to be a good business decision. Now he is planning to take this to other countries as well. Ramon believes that an app like that will be equally popular in Germany as well.

If Satvik had predicted that Paybook would shut down and social media would be deserted, well that did not happen. On the contrary, Paybook users continue to increase even to date. However, Satvik was happy to be proven wrong on this count as it further increased the need for their new venture 'Digital Nirvana'.

About the Author

Sunil is a software professional with over two decades of experience in the field of digital technology. His previous book 'Who Stole My Job' is the story of digital disruption and how it impacts our work lives. Sunil is also the author of 'Transit Lounge' – an Indian's account of travelling to 30 countries.

Currently, Sunil is working with Infosys in India in the area of digital technologies and startup ecosystem. He has earlier worked with McKinsey, Accenture and I-flex solutions.

Sunil is an MBA from IIM-Lucknow and holds a B.Tech from IIT(ISM), Dhanbad.

Website – https://sunilkmishra.com
Twitter - @mishrakrsunil
LinkedIn- in/sunilkrmishra/
Facebook - @authorsunil

Other Books from the Author

"Who Stole My Job?" is a business fiction that captures the tumultuous digital transformation in an Indian IT company trying to re-discover its past glory.

The story captures the journey of a newly hired American CEO through the cultural clash and technology disruption.

"Transit Lounge" is a contemporary book consisting of short incidents, observations and reflections while travelling to 30 countries across six different continents during the last 15 years.